WOLF PACK

Nate idly glanced to his right and felt the short hairs at the nape of his neck prickle. A pair of fiery eyes had left the ring of wolves and was moving toward the tethered mounts and pack animals.

In a flash Nate was on his feet and racing to a point between the advancing wolf and the horses. He slid the whetstone into his possibles bag, draped a hand on one of the flintlocks wedged under his wide brown leather belt, and faced the oncoming predator. "Go away!" he shouted, motioning with his knife hand.

The wolf slowed briefly, then crept nearer. In the forest beyond, others, made bold by the first, were slinking closer.

"I don't like this," Nate muttered.

Shakespeare had risen. "They must be awful hungry."

"Maybe they have a taste for horseflesh," Nate remarked, drawing his pistol. The metallic click of the hammer sounded eerily loud in the dreadful stillness.

"Don't shoot unless you have no other choice," Shakespeare advised. "If you hurt one, the rest will be on us like crazed banshees."

18

WILDERNESS

Mountain Cat
David Thompson

LEISURE BOOKS NEW YORK CITY

To Judy, Joshua, and Shane.

A LEISURE BOOK®

April 1994

Published by

Dorchester Publishing Co., Inc.
276 Fifth Avenue
New York, NY 10001

Printed in the United States of America.

Chapter One

They came silently out of the night, gliding through the dense pine trees to encircle the small clearing where the two men had made their camp. In the glow cast by the crackling fire, only their eyes were visible, fierce crimson slits that lent them the aspect of disembodied demons.

"We have company," announced the older of the two trappers, a grizzled mountain man by the name of Shakespeare McNair. Picking up one of the broken branches collected earlier, he placed it in the flames.

The second man, who was busily honing his long butcher knife, glanced up and scanned the ring of red eyes. "So I see," he said, not at all concerned by the feral arrivals. This man was much younger than the first, much broader of shoulder and with more rippling muscles packed on his hardened frame. Nathaniel King wagged his knife at the newcomers and added, "Should we throw them what's left of our supper?"

"Not unless you want to go hungry tomorrow,"

Shakespeare responded while jabbing a thumb at the pot containing the remainder of their rabbit stew. "That there is breakfast. Let the mangy varmints hunt for their food, like we had to do." Twisting, he cupped a hand to his mouth and bellowed, "Go find someone else to bother!"

None of the eyes so much as blinked.

"Let them watch us if they want," Nate chided. "More often than not, wolves are harmless."

"But not always, as you well know," Shakespeare said. He touched his left shin. "I still have a nasty scar from the time a wolf attacked me when I was toting a dead doe to my cabin."

"I've tangled with them too, on occasion," Nate admitted. "But if this pack doesn't bother me, I won't bother them."

"Getting right peaceable in your young age, are you?" Shakespeare asked, grinning.

"I just see no need to cause trouble where there is none," Nate said. "All I care about is getting this trapping season over with so I can see my family again."

"Spoken like the good husband that you are."

"Are you poking fun at me?"

"Would I do that?" Shakespeare rejoined innocently, and chuckled. "It's just that this old coon isn't hog-tied by apron strings, as are some men I could mention. It doesn't do me any harm to get away by my lonesome every now and then."

"You're trying to get my goat," Nate said, "and it won't work. You, of all people, should know that being in love isn't the same as being hog-tied."

"That depends on the woman," Shakespeare said. "Some wives dig their claws into their men and don't let their husbands so much as breathe without their permission. Others, the smart ones, put their men on a longer leash."

Nate lowered his whetstone and said, "This from the man who is always quoting from *Romeo and Juliet*?"

"You should pay more attention when I do," Shakespeare said, giving a beaded parfleche at his elbow an affectionate pat. In it was the thick volume that had earned McNair his nickname, a book containing the collected works of the Bard of Avon. Shakespeare could recite his namesake by the hour and was often called on by fellow trappers starved for entertainment to do just that. "Here's a quote you must have missed," he commented and coughed to clear his throat. " 'Alas, that love, so gentle in his view, should be so tyrannous and rough in proof!' "

"Shakespeare said that?"

"Old William S. was a heap wiser than most folks give him credit for being."

"Maybe so," Nate said, "but I have a hard time understanding him. It's a shame he couldn't have written in plain English."

"Plain English?" Shakespeare repeated, his eyes sparkling with building mirth. "Where do you think he was from? Spain?"

Nate sighed and touched the edge of his knife to the whetstone. He had been all through this discussion with his mentor before, and he wasn't about to let himself be drawn into another lengthy debate over McNair's literary passion. As he resumed sharpening the blade, he idly glanced to his right and felt the short hairs at the nape of his neck prickle.

A pair of fiery eyes had left the ring of wolves and was moving toward the tethered mounts and pack animals.

In a flash Nate was on his feet and racing to a point

between the advancing wolf and the horses. He slid the whetstone into his possibles bag, draped a hand on one of the flintlocks wedged under his wide brown leather belt, and faced the oncoming predator. "Go away!" he shouted, motioning with his knife hand.

The wolf slowed briefly, then crept nearer. In the forest beyond, others, made bold by the first, were slinking closer.

"I don't like this," Nate muttered.

Shakespeare had risen. "They must be awful hungry."

"Maybe they have a taste for horseflesh," Nate remarked, drawing his pistol. The metallic click of the hammer sounded eerily loud in the dreadful stillness.

"Don't shoot unless you have no other choice," Shakespeare advised. "If you hurt one, the rest will be on us like crazed banshees." Stooping, he grabbed his rifle in one hand and the end of a burning branch in the other. "I'll try to scare them off."

"Be careful."

"Don't fret yourself. I don't intend to end my days in a wolf's belly." Shakespeare waved the firebrand in circles and strode purposefully toward the oncoming wolf. In the flaring radius of light, the beast became clearly visible. It was the apparent leader of the pack, an enormous male sporting a black mask and unusual white markings on its forelegs. The wolf crouched and retreated a few yards, glaring balefully at the firebrand over its shoulder.

"You've got it on the run," Nate said, but, as it developed the very next moment, he had spoken prematurely.

Venting a guttural growl, the leader of the pack suddenly whirled and charged straight at the horse string, streaking across the ground so fast its hairy body was a virtual blur.

Nate instantly fired. In his haste, he missed. The wolf was almost abreast of him, so he took a quick step to the left and slashed with his gleaming knife, causing the pack leader to veer wide. As it did, a rifle boomed and the wolf tumbled. Nate moved in, prepared to dispatch the creature before it could stand. A chorus of snarls stopped him in his tracks.

The majority of the wolves were converging on the camp, their lips drawn back to expose their tapered teeth, their features alight with ferocity.

Dropping the spent pistol, Nate drew his other flint-lock, took a hurried bead on a large specimen, and fired almost at the very same moment that Shakespeare fired a pistol. Two wolves crashed down, one to lie motionless, the other to rise again and limp off.

At the twin blasts, most of the wolves broke off their attack and bolted into the woods. The rest began to circle, seeking an opening.

Nate wanted to reload but feared being set upon while doing so. His Hawken was over by the fire, too far off, for if he ran to retrieve it the poor horses would be unprotected. Instead, he shoved the second pistol under his belt and whipped out his Shoshone tomahawk.

Three wolves were still circling. One darted in close and then darted out into the darkness again, as if daring them to do something or testing their reactions.

Backpedaling to the agitated horses, Nate tried to keep all three wolves in sight at once. A set of eyes disappeared off to his right. Expecting the beast to sneak through an adjacent thicket, Nate dashed to its edge and crouched to peer into the dense vegetation.

McNair, meanwhile, had his hands full with the other two, both of which were padding warily toward the horses but each from a different direction. He had his second pistol out and cocked, and covered first one wolf and then the other, waiting to shoot whichever charged first. If they both charged simultaneously, one was bound to reach the string. Given that wolves regularly hunted large game such as elk and deer and knew how to bring their quarry down by severing leg muscles and tendons, one of the horses might wind up hamstrung, or worse. And every horse was essential. He stepped lightly toward the string, his every nerve tingling.

Over in the thicket, something stirred. Nate tensed, bracing for the rush certain to come. When it did, the wolf sprang with such lightning speed that all Nate could do was bring his tomahawk up to keep the wolf's slavering jaws from closing on his face. Together, they fell backward, the wolf in a frenzy of thwarted blood lust, snapping again and again at Nate's throat. By a sheer fluke, Nate had jammed his forearm under the wolf's chin. He held the beast at bay long enough to bury his knife in the creature's side, the blade spearing in between the wolf's ribs. The wolf yelped and leaped back, almost tearing Nate's arm from its socket. Dripping blood, the knife slipped free. Before Nate could stab a second time, the wolf whirled and fled.

Shakespeare had heard the commotion and glanced around in alarm. To him, Nate King was more like the son he'd never had than just another free trapper, and while he would never admit as much to anyone, he'd gladly sacrifice his own life for the younger man's should the need ever arise. He saw Nate go down and took a few steps towards him. Then he glimpsed one of the wolves racing toward the horses. Pivoting, he snapped off a shot that appeared to strike the wolf in the leg. The wolf went down in a whirl of limbs and tail but bounded up and off without missing a beat. The last wolf followed.

"Nate?" Shakespeare said, running over as the younger man stood. "Are you hurt?"

"No, but it was close," Nate said. "Too close for comfort." His blood pumped madly in his veins and his temples were pounding. He had to clench his fists to keep his fingers from shaking.

"They're gone," Shakespeare announced, surveying the benighted forest. "They were hungry, but not that hungry."

"Hungry enough," Nate grumbled, turning to the horses. His black stallion was the calmest of the bunch, standing with ears pricked and nostrils flaring. The others, including McNair's white mare, whinnied and fidgeted, some pulling at their ropes. Nate moved among them, speaking soft, soothing words and stroking a neck where needed.

Shakespeare was busy reloading his pistols. "We were darned lucky, son. I told you we should have scared those devils off the moment they showed. You'd think that you'd know enough to heed me after all this time."

"Between you and my wife, I should never have to make another decision again," Nate said sarcastically.

" 'Oh, let it not be so! Herein you war against your reputation, and draw within the compass of suspect the unviolated honor of your wife. Once this—your long experience of her wisdom, her sober virtue, years, and modesty, plead on her part some cause to you unknown.' "

"They call it love."

Shakespeare beamed. "I knew you understood old William S. better than you've been letting on."

Their banter was cut short by a piercing howl to the north of their camp, more a wavering wail of despair than the mournful cry so typical of wolves.

David Thompson

"It's one of those we wounded," the mountain man declared.

"We should put it out of its misery."

"It would be downright foolish to go traipsing off through the brush in the dead of night just to finish off a critter that's going to die soon anyway."

Another fluttering wail pierced the night and echoed off the mountains bordering the valley in which they were camped. Many of the peaks were pale, ghostly crags sheathed in white sheets of snow.

"I'll go," Nate proposed.

"We should both stay here," Shakespeare insisted.

"I won't let anyone or anything suffer because of me. It won't take but a few minutes to find the animal and put a ball in its brain."

"What if it still has some fight left? Or there are others still in the vicinity?" Shakespeare shook his head. "You'd be taking too great a risk for no good reason. Let's just sit back down and finish our coffee."

As if to contradict him, the wolf cried a third time, louder and longer than before, a great, sad, pitiable sound that caused Nate's skin to erupt in goose bumps. He went to where his Hawken was propped on his saddle, scooped up the rifle, and headed for the gloomy woods.

"You're being a dunderhead," Shakespeare commented.

"Force of habit," Nate responded, trying to sound carefree and cheery when in fact there were butterflies flitting about in his stomach. A fourth howl drew him into the murk beyond. He proceeded cautiously, bent at the waist with the Hawken tucked to his shoulder, ready for anything.

"If you need help, holler!" Shakespeare called out.

Nate didn't answer. The wolf would hear and know he

was coming. His thumb rested lightly on the Hawken's hammer as he skirted a spruce, passed a boulder, and ducked under a low limb. Away from the fire, the darkness was nearly total. Once his eyes adjusted, his sight would improve a little, but that would take a minute or two.

The undergrowth crackled off to Nate's left and his first thought was that Shakespeare had been right and some of the pack had lingered and were stalking him. Crouching, he waited for whatever was making the noise to appear. To his relief, the animal went the other way and the sounds soon tapered to silence.

Hoping for another howl to guide him, Nate continued deeper into the forest. He set each foot down delicately, as if walking on eggshells, the smooth soles of his moccasins pressing soundlessly onto the thick mat of fallen pine needles that carpeted the earth. His buckskins and his beaver hat blended well into the shadows, making him hard to detect. Unless he blundered, he figured he should be able spot the wounded wolf before it spotted him.

Not ten seconds later, Nate did. He had paused beside an evergreen and leaned against the trunk while scouring the rugged terrain ahead. At the limits of his vision something moved, something low to the ground. Focusing on it, he distinguished a lone wolf crawling on its stomach. From the size of the silhouette, he judged it to be none other than the huge leader of the pack.

Bracing the Hawken against the bole, Nate sighted carefully. Just as he did, the wolf reached high grass and vanished. Thwarted, Nate angled to intercept the beast. At the edge of the grass he stopped, expecting the wolf to soon show itself. Yet time went by, and other than the wind rustling the grass and the leaves of nearby aspens, there was no hint of movement anywhere.

Eager to get back to camp, Nate impatiently crawled into the grass. He held the Hawken in front of him, his palms clammy where they contacted wood or metal. Perhaps, he told himself, Shakespeare had also been right about something else—the stupidity of trying to end the misery of an enraged wild beast that would rip him to shreds without hesitation if it could.

Nate advanced slowly, parting the long stems with his rifle barrel. Even though the crisp mountain air was cool, his brow became dotted with perspiration. His mouth, by contrast, was exceptionally dry. He covered six feet without incident. Eight feet. Ten.

Suddenly a black shape hurtled out of the grass on Nate's left. Twisting, he tried to bring the Hawken to bear but the wolf was on him before he could shoot, its heavy body knocking the rifle aside. Razor-sharp teeth sought his throat. Nate just managed to clamp both hands on the creature's neck as he was bowled onto his back. His shoulders straining mightily, he held the wolf at bay, barely able to retain his grip as the beast snarled and snapped and thrashed.

Drops of saliva fell onto Nate's face. He could feel blood on his fingers and he worried they would become slick and he'd lose his grip. Claws raked his right leg, lancing his body with pain. Nate rammed his knees into the animal's belly, then kicked upward while at the same time he heaved with all his strength. He succeeded in flipping the wolf from him.

Scrambling upright, Nate drew both his knife and his tomahawk a split-second before the wolf closed on him again. It came at his legs but swerved when he tried to cleave its skull with the tomahawk. Rumbling deep in its chest, the wolf then circled him. There was a dark stain on its side but the wound seemed to be having no effect.

Nate had his knife extended and held the tomahawk close to his right shoulder. He turned as the animal circled, always keeping his eyes on it. Somewhere in the nearby grass was his rifle, but he dared not look for it, dared not lower his guard for a moment.

The wolf abruptly sagged, then shook its head and straightened. Apparently the loss of blood was having an effect, but not swiftly enough to suit Nate. He took a gamble and lunged, the tip of his knife catching the wolf on the shoulder as it leaped aside. Incensed, the beast sprang at Nate's legs, and Nate arced the tomahawk at its skull. Exhibiting uncanny reflexes, the wolf evaded the blow and resumed circling.

Nate wanted to kick himself for not taking the time to reload his pistols. How many times had he told his son to never, ever venture into the wild with unloaded weapons? How many times had he pointed out that such forgetfulness could prove fatal? Yet here he'd gone and done the same thing. Sometimes he wondered if he had rocks for brains.

The wolf abruptly charged, and Nate, preoccupied with his thoughts instead of paying attention, jumped to one side too late. He heard the crunch of the wolf's teeth as its jaws closed on his leggings, heard the buckskin tear as the wolf tore into him. Twisting, he speared his butcher knife into its side. The predator jerked back and vented a yelp. Tripping over its own feet, it went down. Nate promptly took a stride, raised the tomahawk on high, and drove it deep into the wolf's skull, connecting as the wolf was in the act of rising. Its head split wide, like a furry cantaloupe. Blood and gore sprayed out.

Nate let go of the tomahawk and sank to one knee.

His pulse was racing again, and he took a minute to calm himself down while observing the wolf's death throes. When the animal finally lay still, he pulled out both the knife and the tomahawk, then wiped them clean on the beast's hide. "You were a tough one," he said softly, standing.

The northwesterly breeze picked up, cooling Nate's brow. Replacing his weapons, he searched until he found the Hawken. Next he stooped, lifted the wolf, and draped its body over his left shoulder. Then he turned his footsteps toward the flickering glow of the fire.

Shakespeare was seated on his blankets, his rifle resting across his legs. He smiled when he saw Nate approaching and lifted his tin cup in a salute. "Well done, son. I was getting a mite worried." His gaze fixed on the wolf. "What do you intend to do with the carcass?"

"Skin it and give the pelt to Winona," Nate said. "Zach has been pestering her for a new hat."

"Had me one made from wolf hide once," the older man mentioned. "It didn't shed water good enough to suit me." Reaching up, he ran a hand over the beaver hat crowning his white hair. It was a perfect match for Nate's own headpiece, except that Shakespeare's wasn't adorned with an eagle feather. "There's nothing like beaver for keeping a man warm and dry."

"True enough," Nate agreed, setting the wolf down next to their supplies. He squatted to examine the tear in his pants and a small cut on his leg. "Any sign of the others?"

"Nope. They high-tailed it elsewhere, and good riddance." Shakespeare nodded at the horses. "If we'd lost them, we'd be up the creek without a paddle."

"I just hope this new territory is all you claim it is," Nate said.

"Would I lie to you?" Shakespeare said indignantly. "I'm telling you the country is crawling with beaver. No white men have been there yet, so we don't have to worry about the streams being trapped out."

"There's a good reason no white men have been there," Nate noted. "It's too close to Blood hunting grounds for anyone to take the risk."

"If we keep our eyes skinned, we should be all right."

Nate hoped so. Dealing with hostile Indians was part and parcel of a trapper's life, but it was a part he could do without. In addition to the Bloods, there were a dozen other tribes that hated all whites; they regarded trappers as invaders deserving torture and death. If the Bloods took him by surprise, he'd suffer a lingering, terrible death.

"Besides," McNair had gone on, "the Bloods should be out on the prairie hunting buffalo at this time of year. It's been a long, hard winter so they're probably low on jerky and pemmican and such. They need a lot of fresh meat and new hides for their lodges. It'll be late Spring or Summer before they move back into the mountains."

"You hope."

Shakespeare arched an eyebrow. "If I'd known you were turning into such a worrier, I would have come alone." He paused. "It's not like you. Why are you so bothered? We've trapped in dangerous territory plenty of times."

"I know," Nate said, shifting to stare northward at a range. "I have a feeling, is all. A bad feeling."

"Bah! You're imagining things! Being a homebody has turned you into a milksop."

"I hope that's all it is," Nate said sincerely, although deep down he wasn't so sure. Was it the chill wind, or was it something else that caused an anxious ripple to course down his spine?

Only time would tell.

Chapter Two

Nate King had an abiding passion for the Rocky Mountains. Ever since he'd initially set foot in them, he'd been entranced by their pristine beauty. The towering, regal peaks, the stark, barren crags, the magnificent forested slopes, verdant valleys, and crystal streams had stirred his soul as no other landscape ever had. And he found that as time went on, to his surprise, he didn't tire of the stirring scenery. Rather, he became even more enamored of the wilderness. He considered it his home, and he would never leave it.

The Rockies always reflected the changing seasons more drastically than Nate's home state of New York ever had. In the fall the aspens glimmered with brilliant hues of red, orange, and yellow, and the grass turned a deep brown. In the winter a white mantle invariably covered everything, lending the terrain a pure, virgin aspect. In the spring, when Nature rekindled the spark of life in the dormant plants and animals, the mountains came alive with all manner of wild creatures and the vegetation flourished. Trees budded and turned green, flowers sprouted and displayed their various beautiful shades, birds chirped gaily, squirrels and chipmunks chattered, and insects buzzed about their daily business.

Paradise on earth, Nate reflected as he wound down a steep slope into the valley where Shakespeare was going to set traps. He could see a wide blue stream half a mile or so off, and grazing near it were a number of elk. Overhead, among pillowy clouds, an eagle soared. To the west, a hawk crested a rocky spire. Sparrows flitted in a fir tree mere yards away. Nate inhaled the pine scented air and smiled in delight.

"No Indian sign anywhere," Shakespeare commented. "We'll have the region all to ourselves."

Nate simply nodded. A boulder the size of a wagon barred his path so he swung to the right, hauling on the lead rope when the foremost pack horse balked. They each had three pack animals, only one of which was burdened with their provisions and traps. The other two would be used later to transport bales of peltries to their cabins.

"It was Broken Paw who told me about this area," Shakespeare said, referring to a Flathead Indian they both knew. "He'd been up here last year hunting and noticed all the beaver dams."

"If there are as many beaver as he claims, when we get back I should give him a gift to show my thanks."

"Don't bother. That crafty coyote already got a knife and some ammo from me for his fusee, as well as a lot of foofaraw and a new blanket for his wife." Shakespeare snickered. "The man drives a hard bargain."

Presently, they came to the valley floor supplies where

Nate spied a game trail and rode along it toward the stream. In the dank earth were imprinted a variety of deep tracks; deer, elk, mountain buffalo, and a fresh set of gigantic prints that caused him to draw rein in consternation. "Grizzly!" he exclaimed.

"Damn. The last thing I want is to get in a racket with one of those monsters."

"That makes two of us," Nate said grimly. By a curious quirk of Fate, it had been his misfortune to tangle with the savage bears frequently. So often, in fact, his bad luck had become a running joke among the trapping fraternity. Nor was his reputation in that regard any better among friendly Indians. Long ago he had been given the name of Grizzly Killer by a Cheyenne who had witnessed his clash with one of the vicious bruins, and now the Shoshones, Flatheads, Crows and other tribes all knew him by that name.

Nate goaded the stallion forward while alertly scanning the valley. He guessed the bear had passed that way sometime since dawn, sometime in the past three hours. It might be long gone. Or it might be hidden in a thicket, dozing. Since grizzlies were prone to attack without warning, he studied the nearest coppices with extra vigilance.

The tracks ended at the stream. Here the bear had either waded to the east or west and the swiftly flowing water had erased all prints.

"Too bad," Shakespeare said. "I was hoping to find out which way the damn thing went."

"We could follow the stream until we find where it came out."

"Why go looking to have our innards ripped out?" Shakespeare said, dismounting. "Leave a grizzly alone and nine times out of ten it'll leave you alone." He glanced up at Nate and grinned. "For most people that's how it works. In your case, grizzlies go out of their way to show you just how nasty they can be. Must be your scent."

"My what?"

"Your scent." Shakespeare stepped to the water's edge, cupped his palm, swallowed a mouthful, and smacked his lips. "Animals have a keen sense of smell. You know that. Some can scent prey a long ways off. Most, when they smell man, head for the hills. But maybe you're special. Maybe there's something about your odor that draws grizzlies like flowers draw bees."

Nate threw back his head and roared. "That has to be the craziest notion you've ever had!"

"Stranger things have happened," Shakespeare said, unruffled. "There are more things in heaven and earth, Horatio, than are dreamt of in your philosophy."

"I don't smell any different from anyone else."

"Care to make a wager?" Shakespeare countered. "The next time you're in a crowded lodge on a hot day, take a few sniffs. See if everyone has the exact same scent or whether they all smell differently."

"I'm not about to go around sticking my nose in armpits to prove you wrong."

"Suit yourself."

Nate slid from the saddle and let his stallion and the pack horses drink. He saw a large fish swimming further out and was tempted to rummage in his pack for his line and hook. But the day was still young and he had a long ride ahead of him if he wanted to reach the next valley before nightfall. "Any idea where you'll make up camp?" he casually inquired.

McNair jabbed a thumb to the west. "I'll set up a lean-to in the trees where hostile eyes won't be likely to spot it." He regarded the gurgling water a moment. "Shouldn't take more than five or six weeks to work a stream this size."

"How about if we meet right at this spot in six weeks then?" Nate suggested.

The mountain man scratched his bushy beard. "Sounds fine, but I still think you should let me take the next valley and you should take this one."

"I lost the toss."

"There's a certain knack to flipping a coin," Shakespeare joked, doing a poor job of concealing his misgivings. "I wouldn't mind switching."

Nate suspected why his mentor was making an issue of a matter already decided. The farther north they went, the closer they would be to Blood territory. "You won fair and square," he reiterated, "so you get to trap this stream and all its branches." To forestall an argument, he stepped into the stirrups and gripped the reins. "Shoot sharps the word."

"Same to you," Shakespeare said rather begrudgingly. "And hold onto that hair of yours."

Bobbing his chin, Nate departed. He jabbed his heels into the stallion and rapidly crossed to the opposite bank. The last pack horse slipped and almost fell but was able to dig in its hoofs and lurch onto firm footing. With a wave, Nate turned his back on his friend and was soon surrounded by woods.

Parting brought a degree of melancholy. Nate liked being with his mentor, liked the company of others. As fond as he was of the mountains, of the remote recesses where few men had ever trod, he wasn't one of those trappers who could go a year or two without seeing another living soul. He wasn't the kind who would rather frolic with wild creatures than with other human beings.

Give Nate his loving family all snug in their sturdy cabin and he was as happy as the proverbial lark. Venturing into parts unknown was exciting, but it was just another aspect to the line of work he had chosen, to the everyday life of a free trapper. Had he been able to collect all the peltries he needed just by walking out his door to the nearest body of water, he would have been perfectly content. But he couldn't. He had to do as other trappers did and seek out the haunts of the beaver.

Once, many years ago, before beaver fur became all the rage in Europe and the States, beaver had existed in great abundance, their lodges decorating every stream of any fair size the length and breadth of the vast Rocky Mountains. Then came the fashion craze and the influx of fur men eager to make their fortunes in the fledgling market. Before long, to the dismay of many Indian tribes, the beaver in wide areas were trapped to extinction.

Now, much to Nate's displeasure, it became harder and harder every season for him to find enough beaver to suit his needs. Every time he went out, he had to travel farther and farther afield, into areas others hadn't thought to penetrate yet, into areas where the risks were higher than he liked.

This particular venture was a case in point. Ordinarily, Nate would have shunned the region he was entering as if the land itself was infested with the plague. He had no inclination to tangle with the Bloods or their allies in the dreaded confederacy that controlled the northern Rockies and plains, the Blackfoot confederacy as it was known since that tribe was its leading member. United with the Piegans, the Bloods and Blackfeet held sway over an area larger than most States, fiercely resisting the influx of whites by exterminating every trapper they encountered.

There were no exceptions to the rule. There were no white men who had been caught and let go again as an act of mercy on the part of the confederacy. If you were white and you fell into the hands of either tribe, you were as good as dead. Every trapper knew it, and every trapper stayed clear of the territory the confederacy claimed as its own.

Even other tribes did the same. The Blackfeet, Bloods, and Piegans were three of the most warlike tribes in all creation. They made ceaseless war on the Crows, the Shoshones, the Flatheads, the Sioux, the Utes. In short, on anyone and everyone who wasn't Blackfoot, Blood, or Piegan. A man might fault their bloodthirsty natures, but there was no denying they slaughtered their enemies fairly, without regard to race or disposition.

Nate had fought warriors from all three tribes on occasion, and the thought of doing so again was enough to cause him to gnaw nervously on his lower lip. A lesser man would have refused to trap in the region they were working. But Nate, despite his reservations, hadn't batted an eye when Shakespeare proposed doing so. Nate had his family to think of. And himself, too. It was his belief that a man did whatever was needed to improve the welfare of those for whom he cared, and if that meant traveling into an area where he was just as likely to lose his life to a wandering grizzly or his scalp to a war party of roving hostiles, so be it.

A man couldn't shirk his responsibility and still wear the label of a man. Not west of the Mississippi, anyway. In the East, in the larger cities in the States, he'd known men who didn't care at all about those who depended on them for a livelihood. Those men would rather spend their evenings at a tavern than with their children, rather spend the night with a soiled dove than with their wives.

Such men didn't know the true meaning of manhood, and Nate had never enjoyed their company.

A meadow appeared ahead, putting an end to Nate's musing. He paused before riding into the open, checking the meadow from end to end and the slopes on either side to be sure no unpleasant surprises awaited him. A trapper could never be *too* cautious.

Nate saw a few black-tailed deer, all does, grazing at a low elevation on the mountain to the east. Across the meadow a solitary magpie pranced about on the ground. There were no bears, no Indians. Reassured, he trotted on, grinning when the magpie rose into the air voicing its distinctive *Mag! Mag! Mag! Mag!*

"A little high up, aren't you?" Nate joked as the magpie flapped into a fir tree. It perched lightly and gave him a cold stare.

"What are you so upset about, you stupid bird?" Nate asked.

And then he saw it. Lying in the grass at the edge of the meadow was a body, not an animal carcass either, but the body of a man dead at least five or six months. Nate immediately reined up and out of pure habit glanced in all directions. Satisfied there was no threat, he climbed down, ground-hitched the stallion, and advanced on tiptoe as if afraid his footsteps would disturb the slumber of the dead.

Nate saw where the magpie had been pecking at tattered ribbons of dried flesh clinging to the skull and felt an impulse to shoot it. He couldn't blame the bird, though. Magpies were greedy feeders, eating anything and everything that caught their fancy. It was magpie nature to peck at corpses.

There was little smell after so much time had elapsed. Still, Nate covered his mouth and nose with a calloused

26

hand and walked around the pale bones, taking note of the few details that might offer a clue to the dead man's identity. Right away he deduced it had been an Indian. The tattered vestiges of a breechcloth clung to the hip bones, as did what was left of a pair of moccasins to the man's feet.

A jagged cavity in the sternum and the fact several ribs had been broken were evidence the warrior had met his end in combat, most likely at the hands of another warrior wielding a tomahawk. Only a tomahawk could cause so much damage to thick human bones. Arrows and knives left nicks and scrape marks. Lead balls left neat furrows or shattered bones into splinters.

Nate couldn't tell which tribe the man had belonged to. His best guess was that a Flathead or Shoshone or some other hunter from one of the friendlier tribes had been caught by a party of Bloods. There were no markings to confirm it, but Nate figured the warrior had been scalped since no self-respecting Blood would pass up such a trophy. There was no trace of torture, although such traces would be hard to discern after all this time unless they were glaringly obvious.

"Poor soul," Nate said, returning to the stallion. Once in the saddle, he by-passed the bones and entered the forest.

The implications of the find were disturbing. Nate had entertained the hope that the valley he would be trapping was far enough south of typical Blood haunts to be spared a visit while he was there. The dead warrior, however, might be proof parties of Bloods did visit the region regularly, perhaps to hunt, perhaps to acquire specific types of wood for their bows, perhaps to gather quartz or rocks used in making arrowheads.

Whatever the reason, the discovery had shattered

Nate's hope and impressed upon him as nothing else could the reality of the dangers he faced. Thinking about them was one thing, finding their potent legacy quite another. His lips compressed into a thin line and he firmed his grip on the Hawken.

For the next several hours Nate wound steadily northward along the base of several mountains and through several emerald hills. Above him reared ivory heights resembling alabaster temples beckoning to lofty deities. Dense growth of spruce and other pines covered the slopes like green cloaks. Everywhere there was wildlife, a teeming variety of animals going about their daily routines in characteristic style. Some, such as the big gray squirrels and ravens, were noisy to the point of being pests. Others, such as rabbits and raccoons, were so quiet a man didn't know they were there until he spooked them. Then there were the larger animals usually seen only from a discreet distance, such as the elk and the noble bighorn sheep.

Nate never tired of admiring the spectacle. During his early years, he'd been fascinated to the depths of his being by accounts in books written by explorers and missionaries of the countless kinds of exotic animals found in distant places such as Africa and Asia. Never in a million years would it have occurred to him that he could find the very same thing on the North American continent.

Wasn't that the human way, though? Nate asked himself. As the old saying went, the grass always looked greener on the other side of the fence. Natural wonders might be right in front of a person's face, but they'd never see them if they were too busy craning their necks for a glimpse of the far horizon. How odd that so few recognized the truth.

Once past the mountains and among the hills, Nate was troubled to note the animals all fell silent. Silence wasn't Nature's normal state. A profound quiet served as a sure sign of looming peril. The cause might be something as simple as the advent of a severe thunderstorm, or it might have a more sinister genesis: prowling predators, whether four-legged or two-legged.

Nate rode uneasily, shifting often to survey the impenetrable woods. Pines, when clustered close, formed a seemingly solid wall capable of hiding a full-grown grizzly or an entire war party. Many a trapper had lost his life when set on without warning by an enemy that appeared almost at his very elbow, too late for the trapper to do more than blink. Nate had no intention of being one of them.

The hills gave way to a low ridge that formed a barrier between them and the valley. Here a whole slope had been devastated by a lightning strike resulting in a widespread fire that reduced thousands of patriarchs of the forest to mere charred fragments and stumps. The ground had been darkened by the inferno but was now sprinkled with islands of hardy grass.

Nate threaded among gnarled black steeples and around ebony logs once home to thriving insects and birds and animals but now reduced to pitted, lifeless hulks. There wasn't so much as a solitary chipmunk abroad on the blistered slope.

At the top, Nate stopped and breathed in relief, glad to be up where the air lacked an acrid taint and the trees rustled with vitality. His breath caught short when he gazed out over the valley he would call home for the next six months. There were valleys, and there were *valleys*.

Ages past, a giant cyclops must have taken a crooked

scythe to the land, creating a deep, ugly scar that had healed in the course of time and resulted in a valley with so many twists and bends that from high in the air it must have the appearance of a knotted snake. The faces of the ringing mountains to the north, east, and west were strangely barren and so inclined that they shielded the valley floor from much of the sunlight that would otherwise penetrate.

A cool breeze wafted up and out over the ridge, making Nate shiver. He shook himself, turned the stallion, and moved along the ridge eastward, giving his new home a thorough inspection. A wide stream was visible, which confirmed there would be beaver. Or should be, at any rate. No other animals were in sight, which in itself wasn't remarkable. Early afternoon was a time for deer and elk to lay low in thickets and the meat eaters to rest up for their nightly hunting.

That reminded him. Nate squinted up at the sun, judging he had five or six hours of daylight remaining. Less in the valley, where the peaks to the west would cause an artificial sunset an hour or so earlier. He had to hurry.

Ten minutes of looking failed to reveal a game trail, so Nate made his own, picking his downward course with care, keenly aware he couldn't afford to lose a single horse. The incline was steep, in spots almost severe. It required an hour to gain the valley floor.

Birds were singing again when Nate trotted on a beeline for the stream. The temperature was cooler, but that would be an advantage when he began working hard. He heard the bubbling of rapid current before he broke from the pines onto a grassy strip bordering the source of his livelihood. As with the majority of high mountain streams, the water in this one seemed in an almighty hurry to get to a lower elevation. A stick went flashing past, bobbing with the ebb and flow.

Nate turned westward. Beaver didn't make their lodges in the middle of rapids. They needed still water. Which was no doubt why they spent most of their adult lives building and rebuilding the dams so critical to their existence. In a sense, beaver had a set of responsibilities similar to his own. The fate of their families rested on their ability as providers and protectors. It was a bit sad, Nate reflected, that the latest fashion craze hadn't been chicken feathers instead.

Around a bend was a sight so glorious that Nate quivered with excitement: a tremendous dam, the work of generations of beaver, built at a critical point, an ideal spot to stem the rapid flow without causing so much pressure to build up during times of flood that the dam would be swept away. Over the top cascaded the overflow, re-forming at the bottom into the current contributing to the rapids.

Nate rode past the immense jumbled bowl of trunks, limbs, and odds and ends. A tranquil pond unfolded before him. All along the shore were recently felled trees or the upthrust spikes of those downed long ago. A dozen feet out from the bank rose the hump forming the roof of the lodge. There was no sign of activity, and there probably wouldn't be until later. In the early evening beaver came out to treat themselves to fresh bark and inspect their dams, while most of the actual construction work was done at night.

Going on, Nate presently discovered another dam. And another. There was so much beaver sign, in his mind's eye he was already seeing the thick bales of prime pelts he would be taking to the next rendezvous. At a muddy stretch flanking a straight section of rushing water, he saw something else, something that made him jerk on the reins so hard the stallion titled its head quizzically.

The mud bore dozens of tracks, some old, some new, testimony to the drinking habits of a variety of creatures. Most prominent were the telltale pad marks of the one animal able to hold its own against a riled grizzly, the pad marks of what had to be the biggest panther in all existence.

Chapter Three

That first night in the new valley Nate slept in a small clearing at the base of a cliff located almost a full mile north of the stream. With the rock wall at his back, he only had to worry about something coming at him from the front. He gathered several loads of dry wood, bedded down the horses close to the cliff, and spread out his blankets between them and the fire. The long day on the trail had left him too tired to bother hunting his supper. He settled for some of the pemmican his wife had thoughtfully packed.

As Nate munched, he pondered. The gigantic panther tracks weren't much cause for alarm since the big cats were known to roam over a wide range and the one responsible for the prints might not show up in the valley again for many days, if not weeks. And when it did, the odds were that the panther, or mountain lion as a few of the trappers had taken to calling the breed, would just go about its business without bothering him.

Like wolves, panthers normally wanted nothing to do with humans.

Seated there close to the crackling flames, warm and content and drowsy, Nate felt a bit ashamed of his earlier misgivings. The valley was really no different from any other. Oh, its shape was extraordinary, but it still had a stream and grass and trees, just as others did. And while the surrounding peaks tended to shade the valley floor more hours of the day than was typical, shade in and of itself was hardly sinister. He laughed at his former feelings and took a swig of piping hot coffee.

Nate knew how a mind could play tricks on a person, especially in the rugged Rockies where the awe-inspiring landscape was a heady spectacle that stirred the emotions to undreamt of heights. The imagination was free to soar with the eagles, and if left unchecked, might soar into stormy clouds of worry and despair. Many a trapper had fallen prey to the ravings of his own mental fancies, and Nate had no intention of joining their ranks.

There had been one man in particular whose story Nate recalled vividly. The trapper, a greenhorn from North Carolina or some such Southern state, had outfitted himself in Missouri and traveled west with a rendezvous caravan. At the annual gathering he'd announced to all and sundry that he was going to bring back more furs the next year than any trapper had ever done before. And off he went to trap on his own. A few of the men offered to be his partner, but he'd refused each and every one.

The next rendezvous came along and the Southerner failed to show. Some wondered about the loud greenhorn, speculating on his possible fate. Indians, a wild beast, a natural disaster like an avalanche, or an innocent accident might have cost the brash youngster his life.

Mountain Cat

Hundreds of trappers perished every year from those common hazards, and others.

Afterward, the North Carolinian was forgotten about until later that fall when a group of trappers riding into unknown land to the west found a crude cabin near a high pass. Bleached bones of horses long dead dotted the weeds choking the front of the structure. Inside they found human bones, a single skeleton in a heap beside a chair. They also uncovered a journal.

Evidently, the greenhorn had come on an area rich with beaver and decided to winter there. He'd built the cabin from downed trees, stored his bales inside, stocked up on jerky, and prepared to wait until Spring to head east. About halfway through the winter, however, the isolation got to the man.

His journal related the entire story. At first, the trapper complained of being spied on by unseen eyes. He thought he was being watched as he went about his daily chores, and he was certain hostiles were sizing him up to take his hair. Then he began hearing peculiar noises, mostly at night, scratching and rustling and low whispering. Yet when he dashed outside to confront the intruders, no one was there.

Several weeks of this ordeal had a terrible effect on the trapper's fraying mental state. He wrote in his journal of seeing large, strange bugs crawling about in the forest behind his cabin and of hearing them on his roof after dark. He'd shoot at them, to no avail. He'd rail at them, and throw sticks and stones, but they refused to leave.

Finally came the day when the trapper barricaded himself inside. In his journal he told of a fierce seige by the bugs, and how he was valiantly fighting them off. Some, though, were getting in through cracks in the walls or chinks in the floor and crawling up under his buckskins to bite and tear at his flesh. He was doing the best he could to resist the dark tide, but he labored at a disadvantage since many of the bugs were invisible.

The trapper's last entry spoke eloquently of his abject state. He'd stripped off his clothes so the bugs couldn't hide on his person. He'd stabbed himself a few times in the belief he was stabbing attacking bugs. Desperate, in terrible agony, he'd decided to put an end to himself before the bugs crawled into his mouth and nose and ears and ate his innards, burrowing from the inside out. The man had sat in a makeshift chair, cocked a pistol, stuck the tip of the barrel in his mouth, and squeezed the trigger. Simple as that.

Nate had seen the journal and touched the drops of blood scattered over its last two pages. He remembered wondering if the same fate would one day befall him, remembered scoffing at the idea. Yet he had behaved the same way at sight of the valley.

Now, staring into the comforting fire, Nate grinned and slapped his leg, amused by his foolish behavior. It was all right for kids to be afraid of the dark and other imaginary demons; they didn't know any better. But he was a grown man. He'd slain grizzlies, wolverines, and Apaches. He had nothing to fear but fear itself.

Later that night, snug under his blankets, his head propped on his hands, his gaze on the multitude of sparkling stars, Nate laid his plans for the next day. In the distance a coyote yipped, closer by an owl voiced its unique question. Gradually he drifted into dreamland and was on the verge of deep slumber when he heard something which made him sit bolt upright and grab for his Hawken.

From the west, from farther up the valley, wafted a menacing, guttural snarl totally unlike those of the wolves. It was deeper, louder, more ferocious, resembling muted thunder more than anything else, an elemental sound that inspired elemental dread.

Nate listened breathlessly. When the snarl died, he laid back down and tried telling himself the incident was of no consequence. So what if the panther was still in the valley? So what if it was on the prowl? He reminded himself that panthers seldom attacked people. To be on the safe side, though, he added fuel to the fire until the blaze was twice the size it had been. Then he reclined on his side, facing the woods, and cupped a palm around a pistol.

Sleep was a long time claiming him.

A pink glow tinged the eastern sky when Nate woke up and heated the coffee left over from the evening before. The strong brew and jerky sufficed for breakfast. His saddle went on the stallion, his parfleches and packs on one of the pack horses, and off he rode, savoring the tangy nip in the air. On all sides birds serenaded the rising sun.

Morning was one of Nate's favorite times. It gave him a wholesome sense of renewal, of starting each day with a clean slate. He looked forward to the work he had to do, and to raising his first beaver. In a few days he would have some pelts ready to sell. In six weeks he would have bales of them.

First things first. Nate watered the horses, then rode westward, noting the locations of lodges and spots where trees had recently been felled. Midway up the valley he established his permanent camp in a sheltered clearing bordered by thickets on two sides, dense spruce on the third, and the stream on the fourth.

Taking a half-dozen traps, Nate retraced his route

and placed them at suitable points. Most went close
to lodges, others near runs made by the beaver when
leaving or entering the water. He had to wade out into
the stream, then position the set traps deep enough under
the surface to drown the animals when caught. Each
trap was baited with castorum, a yellow substance taken
from their glands. The scent drew beavers like flowers
drew bees.

Done with the first batch, Nate went back to camp and
spent the next two hours erecting a sturdy lean-to, angled
so it blocked the prevailing northwesterly winds. Some
trappers liked to build their shelters of hides, but Nate
considered the practice a horrible waste of prime fur.

The frame for stretching pelts was Nate's subsequent
chore. He used firm, trimmed limbs and lashed them
together with whangs from his buckskins. A graining
block had to be set up. And when that was done, Nate
piled a store of wood.

Plenty of daylight remained, so Nate took his sack of
Newhouses and went westward along the stream placing
trap after trap. Newhouse was the name of the man
who manufactured the traps, and many now called his
product by his name. In additions Newhouse published a
manual known as *THE TRAPPERS GUIDE,* a somewhat
misleading book that had lured countless gullible souls to
the mountains in search of fortune. Newhouse claimed
trapping was a 'gentlemanly' occupation, and proved
it by illustrating his guide with drawings of so-called
trappers in refined city clothes doing things like skinning
beaver and shooting game.

Still, the man made a fine steel trap. He'd wisely
designed the jaws to be smooth, not jagged, so the
fur wouldn't be damaged. A disk at the bottom was
the trigger that caused the leaf springs to fly up and

lock the jaws in place. It all happened so fast, there was no time for an animal to pull its foot from harm's way once the disk was stepped on.

Nate had to be careful. Quite a few trappers had lost thumbs or fingers after accidentally snaring their own hands in the snapping jaws. A moment's distraction was all it took. He'd learned to concentrate on the trap and nothing but the trap when setting the trigger and lowering the device into the water.

Sixteen traps Nate was able to put out that afternoon. The sun crowned the mountains when he tied his sack to his saddle and trotted back to camp. Along the way, he double-checked to be sure he had blazed trees near each of the traps so he could find them again.

That night Nate ate rabbit stew spiced with wild onions and herbs. He treated himself to sugar in his coffee to celebrate the laying of his line. His dreams that night were of piles and piles of glossy peltries.

The next day was a repeat of the first. Nate succeeded in placing nearly half of his traps by sunset, and that evening, when making his rounds, he found the first snared beaver, a husky male with a lustrous coat. The animal had tried to bite its leg off to escape but fortunately failed.

By the end of the fourth day all the traps had been set out and Nate had his hands full tending to the hides of those caught. It always happened that more beaver were caught right after a trap line was laid out than later on. Once the beaver population started to dwindle, the survivors exercised more caution, steering clear of anything that smelled of man or metal. A trapper had to use more ingenuity in order to keep on catching them.

Nate had no such problem for the time being. Day after day went by, each rewarding him with five or six more beaver. His routine was always the same. Up at dawn to eat a hurried breakfast, a check of all the traps to retrieve any animals caught overnight, each of which had to be lugged to camp, then the late morning and early afternoon hours were spent working on pelts. Late afternoon was devoted to another patrol of the stream. Finally came supper, and more curing and scraping until he was too tired to stay awake another minute.

In this way four weeks elapsed. Nate lost all track of time, he was so immersed in his work. He trapped the main stream out and started on several branches where younger beaver had been driven by population pressure to establish their own lodges. Not once did Nate see another human being. Animals were his sole companions in the remote valley, deer and elk and countless smaller creatures.

Nate loved every minute. He often thought of his former job as an aspiring accountant in New York City, and he marveled that he had once seriously considered spending the rest of his life chained to a desk. He remembered the small work area he'd been given, and being huddled over ledgers late into the night to get caught up for a client. He remembered the reek of the lamps, the sore eyes, the cramps in his back. How could he have been so stupid?

All Nate had to do was pause and gaze at the majestic splendor all around him to see his former folly for what it had truly been. Give him the invigorating mountain air, spiced with the earthy scent of pine! Give him the deep blue sky, the rich brown earth and deep green forests! Give him the freedom to live as he damn well pleased instead of having to bow to every whim of a fickle employer! This was the life! The only life!

Early on, Nate forgot about the panther, forgot about

his premonition, forgot about his feelings of unease. Trapping took all his time from sunrise to midnight. There weren't any idle moments to spend in worthless musing. Gradually his collection of peltries grew and grew, and after a month he was the proud owner of one hundred and five hides.

Everything went extremely well until the day Nate approached his camp with a forty-pound beaver slung over a shoulder and heard his horses nickering. By their tone Nate realized they were upset. Grasping his Hawken tighter, he jogged the rest of the way and came to the edge of the clearing in time to glimpse a tawny form vanishing into the thicket on the other side. So fleeting was the glimpse that Nate couldn't be sure if he'd seen a panther, a bobcat, or something else entirely.

The black stallion was nervously prancing back and forth. Dropping the beaver, Nate ran over and calmed the troubled horse before it could break loose from its tether. He scoured the underbrush but saw no sign of their visitor. Not satisfied, he tiptoed into the thicket and crouched low to the ground where he would be more likely to spot movement. The still plants mocked him. Whatever had been there was apparently gone.

Nate searched in vain for tracks, thanks to the hard soil and the thick grass. He made a circuit of the camp to see if the animal had left prints elsewhere and was disappointed to find none.

Vaguely troubled, Nate resumed working. The horses hadn't been harmed and none of his belongings had been disturbed, so he shouldn't be worried. Yet he couldn't shake a persistent, nagging, trifling sense of impending trouble.

Butcher knife in hand, Nate set the beaver on its back and slit down the back of each hind leg. Cutting slowly, he opened a straight slit from the chin to the tail. Then, using his fingers, he peeled the beaver's hide down over its head as he might peel a stocking from his foot. While peeling he had to cut ligaments and muscles holding the hide in place, remembering to always hold the edge of the knife slanted toward the body and not toward the hide to avoid nicking the valuable fur.

While the hide was still pliable, Nate attached it to the stretching frame he had made. A rough stone sufficed as a scraper, and with it he removed shreds of muscles and fat that had clung to the inside of the pelt. He also trimmed off a few ragged edges. Overall, though, the hide was as fine as any he'd ever collected.

That evening Nate half expected the horses to get the scent of something and act up again, or to hear the throaty cry of the giant panther. Neither occurred. Bad nerves again, he figured, and turned in when the fire was so low it was almost out.

What woke Nate up, he couldn't say. One second he was sound asleep, the next he was lying there in near total darkness listening to his horses stomp and nicker. Instantly he pushed erect, rifle tucked to his shoulder. The snap of a twig to the west showed him which way to turn, and as he did he saw something at the edge of the spruce trees. He took a hasty bead, wishing he could see the thing clearly, when it suddenly disappeared. Puzzled, he bent at the waist and dashed forward.

Nate reached the thicket and halted. He glanced right, he glanced left. There was no sign of the creature. The horses were even more agitated now, the stallion trying to rear, one of the pack horses tugging furiously at its rope.

"Damn," Nate muttered. He had no choice but to dash to the horses and try yet again to quiet them down. The stallion did so immediately but the pack horse was in a panic, forcing Nate to seize the tether and hold fast to stop the animal from trying to break free.

In the thicket to the east arose a faint rustling.

Nate twisted, whipping the Hawken up with one hand. He realized the nocturnal prowler had circled completely around his camp. Was it the huge panther? Or something else? The pack horse continued to strain against him and he was of half a mind to pound the rifle stock onto its thick skull to teach it a lesson, but he had never been one to brutalize animals and wasn't about to start.

The rustling ceased. An eerie stillness gripped the gloomy forest. All Nate could hear was the sighing of the wind in the trees and the soft purling of the stream. Giving the rope a last pull to show the pack horse who was boss, he darted to his blankets and hastily crammed his pistols, knife, and tomahawk under his belt. Then, donning his hat, he sped into the thicket to the east, making no attempt to move stealthily in the hope he would flush the beast.

A flitting hint of a flashing inky shadow was the only clue Nate had to the creature's location. He promptly veered toward it, but whatever the animal was, it easily outdistanced him, racing off with a speed even the black stallion would be hard pressed to match. Into the adjacent woods it ran, and there, oddly, it paused in the open and seemed to look back.

Nate sprinted in pursuit. As yet he had not had a clear view of the thing. The general shape, though, and its fluid, incredibly swift movements were consistent with those of a panther. He was within twenty feet of the creature and raising the Hawken when once again the animal fled.

In the act of slowing since he had no chance at all of

catching it, Nate was mildly surprised when the cat—if such it was—stopped once more and looked back. The inexplicable behavior confused him. Was the panther taunting him or merely curious? Whichever, he couldn't afford to let a panther skulk about his camp at will and perhaps eventually bring down one of his horses when temptation proved too much to resist. So he pressed on, his thumb resting on the Hawken's hammer.

The big cat let him approach within twenty-five feet, then wheeled and flowed like quicksilver further into the trees. Yet it only ran another thirty feet or so when it halted again.

Nate was thoroughly confounded. He'd never heard tell of any panther behaving as this one was doing. The only explanation he could think of was that the cat had seldom if ever seen a human being and wasn't sure whether he was a threat or not. In a way he regretted having to dispatch it. He slowed, thinking the cat would be less likely to run off, and lowered the Hawken to his side.

The panther waited until Nate was less than twenty feet away, then spun and glided into undergrowth to the south. Nate hurried to the vegetation and sank to one knee, seeking a target. Darkness and bushes were all he saw. Frustrated, he moved a few yards to the left to vary the angle. Somewhere in there the cat was hiding. He was sure of it.

But Nate was wrong.

A minute had gone by when frightened whinnies brought Nate to his feet in dismay. His gut balled into a knot as he perceived that the panther had circled once again, this time back to the clearing, back to the horses. Nate flew toward the camp, his moccasins slapping the earth in regular cadence. The whinnies grew more strident, loudest among them the deep cries of the stallion. But where the pack horses, all mares, were neighing out of fear, the stallion was in a fury. Nate prayed the black wouldn't tear loose and fight the cat. The stallion was one of the best horses he had ever owned and he didn't care for anything to happen to it.

Suddenly the whinnies of the stallion took a new, harsher tenor, and mingled with the stallion's snorts and bellows were the low growls of an angry cat.

Nate's worst fear had come to pass. He could distinguish the stallion through the thicket, rearing and kicking in wild abandon, the firelight highlighting the rippling muscles under its satiny coat. Clutching the rifle in both hands, he plunged into the thicket and barreled his way through to the clearing, there to behold a sight few men had ever witnessed.

The black stallion was engaged in mortal combat with a panther of such immense proportions it appeared more like a monster from prior ages than a mountain lion. Long of body, unnaturally thick through the middle, and powerfully endowed with bulging sinews, the cat was easily evading the stallion's flailing hoofs. It leaped from side to side with effortless ease, its ears flattened against its round head, its lips curled to reveal its wicked teeth. At any second it might see an opening and pounce.

"No!" Nate roared, closing. Here was the clear shot he needed and he was going to take it, but as he brought the Hawken to bear the panther streaked out of the clearing to the west, a molten blur impossible to hit.

Nate cursed and stopped. He wasn't going to make the same mistake twice and follow the cat into the forest. Simmering with baffled wrath, he glanced at the stallion, which was standing still, its sides heaving, its eyes fixed on the spot where the panther had entered the spruce trees.

"Well now," Nate declared bitterly, "this changes everything, big fellow. I'm not about to leave this valley until I'm done trapping, so I guess that means we're in for a heap of trouble." He shook the rifle at the trees and repeated softly, "A heap of trouble."

Chapter Four

Old Satan.

As the story related time and again over the years went, some of the very first trappers ever to set foot in the Rocky Mountains ran into a bestial fiend that qualified as Evil Incarnate. Four hardy men from Pennsylvania had gone into unexplored territory despite warnings from friendly Shoshones to stay away from the region for fear of encountering the legendary Devil Beast. The whites had understandably scoffed at the silly notion of a panther renowned for ferocity unmatched by any living creature, a panther that had lived more scores of years than any man could remember, that had been shot with arrows time and again and pierced by lances and knives and yet lived on unharmed.

Into the unknown the quartet went, and they paid dearly for neglecting to take the Shoshones seriously. One of the men was pounced on while he slept and dragged off into the brush. When the body was found by his companions the next day, it was scattered in small pieces as if the panther had ripped it to shreds in wanton feline glee.

The remaining three had packed up and headed out of the country, but the panther wasn't about to let them go. It shadowed them for days, often showing itself beyond rifle range and keeping them awake at night with its unearthly screams. Their horses were driven off, never to be seen again.

A second trapper lost his life when he heeded Nature's call and forgot to keep one eye behind him. This man had his head shorn from his body and his entrails clawed out.

Days later the two weary survivors took their only good shot at their tormentor. Both were experienced woodsmen. Both were excellent shots. Yet, somehow, both missed, because the panther simply stared at them for a few moments after the thunder of the gunshots receded in the distance and then calmly walked off as if taking a stroll in a city park.

Miles from the Shoshone village one of the trappers, worn out from lack of food and sleep, stopped to rest on a log while his companion hastened ahead for help. When the rescue party arrived, the only article of the trapper's on the log was his rifle. A smear of blood led the last trapper and the warriors into a glade where the torso of the hapless dead man was found. His arms and legs, however, were missing.

Thus started the undying saga of Old Satan. The sole survivor told other trappers, and they in turn passed on the story, and so on and so on until every trapper became familiar with it. Trappers loved to talk, to swap tall tales around their campfires, and no tale was more popular than that of the monster panther. Somewhere along the line the cat received a fitting name. Now and then others would claim to have seen it but no one believed them. Monstrous panthers simply didn't exist.

Now Nate knew better.

The story came to mind the next morning as Nate was saddling the stallion to go make his rounds of the traps. He had decided to take his horses with him every time he left camp. It was either that or risk losing one and he needed them all to pack out his plews. Sliding a loop over the neck of the lead pack animal, he rode into the rising sun, staying close to the water's edge so he could see if the traps had done their job.

Less than a hundred feet from the clearing Nate came on a gravel bar rimmed with mud bearing the same enormous tracks he'd seen previously. The panther had squatted to lap the cold water, then leaped from the end of the gravel bar to the far bank, a jump of eighteen feet.

Nate resumed his morning routine. Four beavers had to be transported back to camp and skinned. That evening he made his second sweep, and this time he made a shocking discovery.

A wide tributary of the main stream contained two lodges. Nate had already trapped the nearest. The second was in a ravine gouged into the side of a neighboring mountain where the ravine widened and the runoff from on high formed a serene pool. A narrow strip of solid footing between the sheer face of the ravine and the water had permitted Nate to get close enough to the lodge to plant his traps.

Now, as Nate dismounted at the mouth of the pool and hiked along its perimeter toward the lodge, he noticed a strange crimson tint to the water flowing sluggishly by. He stared at the red stain until its meaning hit him like a ton of falling boulders. Then he broke into a run.

David Thompson

Two of the traps had contained beaver. One trap had been dragged, stake and all, clear out of the pool. The other was at the bottom, lying on its side. In the jaws of both dangled the shorn legs of the beavers.

Nate clenched his fists in rage and scanned the ravine from one end to the other. The panther was long gone but its handiwork was impossible to miss; the pair of beaver had been ripped apart, their organs, limbs, and hides forming a gory mess at the base of the wall. From the evidence, Nate doubted any of the meat had been eaten. The panther had done it for the sheer hell of it.

A cat that would enter water? Nate recalled hearing of panthers seen fording rivers, but he was under the impression they only got wet if there was no alternative. This one was different. It had deliberately gone in after the beavers, as if it had made the connection between Nate and the traps and knew that killing the catch would anger him.

That was a crazy idea! Nate told himself. Animals couldn't think, at least not the same way people did. An animal acted out of instinct and reflex. Complex plotting was beyond them. Everyone knew that. But how else could he explain the deaths of the beavers?

Nate gathered the traps and opened the jaws of each so the imprisoned legs fell out. Slinging the Newhouses by their chains over his shoulder, he walked to the horses and secured the traps to one of the pack horses. Not without some difficulty, because the horse's sensitive nostrils picked up a whiff of blood and it shied.

The ride to the camp was spent in somber thought. Nate hadn't trapped all of the tributaries yet. Making a rough guess, he pegged the total number of beaver still to be caught at forty. Enough for a new rifle for his son, or a lot of foofaraw for his wife and daughter. He wasn't inclined to pass that many pelts up.

Which left Nate with the pressing problem of how to deal with Old Satan, as he had taken to calling the beast. Tracking it down would take too much time, make him late for his reunion with Shakespeare. He didn't have poison or he'd bait a dead beaver and let the cat's own bloodthirsty nature do it in. Snares and other kinds of traps would probably be useless against such a wily creature. So what was left?

One thing was for sure. Nate couldn't tolerate having the beaver butchered. Yet he also couldn't be everywhere at once. While he was checking downstream, the panther might be upstream wreaking havoc, or just the opposite. Somehow he had to draw the cat within range of his Hawken.

Easier thought than done. How, Nate wondered, was he to lure in an animal as naturally wary as a mountain lion? What would interest it? A low nicker behind him gave him the answer, and he shifted in the saddle to regard the three pack horses. The scheme was fraught with risk, but if he did it right, it just might work.

Nate plotted the rest of the ride. He ate beaver meat for supper, then walked close to the stream where the soil was softest and began scooping dirt with a broken limb. Sweat was trickling down his back by the time he had a suitable depression excavated. With an eye on the setting sun, he accumulated brush from the thicket and piled it next to the depression.

Picking the pack horse was easy. Nate chose the one that had given him the hardest time since leaving home. Gripping its lead rope, he escorted the mare to the stream bank and fastened the rope to a log too heavy for the mare to drag off. He took measured paces from the log to the depression, counted fifteen, and nodded in satisfaction. Ideal range.

The stallion and the other two mares were tied within spitting distance of the blaze. They disliked being so close, but it was either that or leave them in the dark at the mercy of the panther.

Nate sat and sipped black, strong coffee for the next hour. He might need to stay awake all night and the brew would help. All was quiet during that time, except for the horse by the stream which kept whinnying. It was upset at being separated from the others and didn't like being left in the dark.

Presently Nate threw enough limbs on the fire to last for hours and went to the depression. Lying on his side so he was facing the decoy, he then covered himself with the brush until he was completely concealed. From a distance the blind should fool Old Satan.

Now all Nate could do was wait. He set the rifle in front of him, shifted onto his stomach, and rested his chin on his forearms. A mild breeze fanned the tops of the trees, and off to the right a cricket chirped.

Would Satan come? That was the burning question. Nate hoped he wouldn't wind up staying awake all night and then not get a shot at the cat. Losing sleep was a sacrifice he could ill afford, not with all the work yet to be done before he could leave the valley, but going without would be well worth it if he bagged the panther.

The minutes dragged by, becoming a full hour. The mare continued to whinny every so often. On occasion the stallion answered her. Several times she threw her weight against the rope, which held fast.

Nate did his best to stay fully awake and alert, but despite his best intentions his mind strayed. Fatigue and the deceptive quiet lulled him into a drowsy state. Memories washed over him, memories long forgotten. . . . or avoided.

Another time, another place.

In a newly painted frame house in a well-to-do section of New York City, a boy of twelve was on his bed, his head propped on his pillow, reading a book. Into his room stalked a square-jawed man with eyes the hue of flint.

"Here you are. I should have known you'd be wasting your time, as always."

The boy lowered the book and dutifully sat up. "I'm not wasting my time, Father. I'm reading."

"Reading what, as if I can't guess?" the father responded. He took the book from the boy and examined the cover, his mouth scrunched up as if he had just tasted a bitter lemon. "*Prometheus Unbound* by Percy Bysshe Shelley. Why do you read this drivel?"

"Poetry is good for the soul, father."

"Where did you ever get such a silly idea? From your mother? The woman should stick to her knitting and cooking and stop trying to turn you into a hopeless romantic." The father flipped a page and started reading. "My soul is an enchanted boat, which, like a sleeping swan, doth float upon the silver waves of—" He glanced up, shook his head in disgust, then tossed the offending volume to the floor. "Enough. I won't have you reading such trash."

"But, Father—"

"But nothing." The man gripped the boy's arm and pulled him off the bed. "Listen to me, and listen closely. I have a job for you to do and I want it done right."

"What sort of job?" the youngster asked. "I already did my chores."

"Don't give me sass, son," the father warned. "Come with me and I'll show you."

They walked without speaking down the hall, down the stairs, and along another hall to the kitchen. In the corner near the stove the father halted and pointed. "There."

The boy looked but only saw the white wall and the polished baseboard. "There what?"

"At the bottom, by the stove. Don't you see it?"

There was a small hole in the baseboard, no bigger than the boy's thumb. "That?"

"Kill it."

"Sir?"

"I want you to kill it."

"Kill what?" the boy asked, although he knew full well.

"The mouse, dunderhead. What else?" Scowling, the father motioned at a nearby table. "Your mother saw one this morning when she was setting the silverware out. About gave her a heart attack." A thin smile transformed his scowl. "You know how women are. Afraid of their own shadows."

The boy barely heard. "You want *me* to do it?"

"Why not you?" the father rejoined sternly. "Your brothers have other jobs to do. And you certainly don't expect me to devote precious time to so simple a task? A girl could do this."

"I've never killed a mouse before."

"It's easy. Set some cheese out and when the dirty little rodent shows itself, bash its brains in."

"I've never killed *anything* before."

The father sighed. "So? It's about time you did then,

isn't it? You're too squeamish for your own good. Why, when I was your age, I regularly chopped the heads off chickens and often helped my father. slaughter hogs. Sometimes I waded in blood and gore up to my ankles, but it was great fun."

The boy bit his lower lip.

"Do you know what your problem is? I've been too damn easy on you, spared you from life's realities. And those ridiculous poetry books don't help matters any. Life isn't all sugar and spice, son. You must learn to take the sour with the sweet." The father strode to the wood box and selected a stout length of firewood. "Here."

"You want me to use that?"

"You can kick the mouse to death for all I care," the father said, shoving the bludgeon into his son's hands. "But this will work nicely. Just remember to smash it in the head. I don't want its guts spread all over the floor. Your mother won't like that one bit."

The boy stared at the club and gulped. "I'll do my best, father."

"Of course. I knew I could rely on you."

The mare whinnied for the hundredth time, only this time there was a new note, a high-pitched quality that snapped Nate out of his reverie and returned him to the present. He automatically lifted his head and accidentally rustled the brush covering him. Freezing, he gazed at the mare and saw her staring out across the stream.

Was Satan coming? Had the cat taken the bait? Nate probed the night, his finger on the trigger of his rifle. He must be ready to fire at an instant's notice in order to protect the mare. She moved and stared to the northwest. Nate did the same yet was unable to spot the mountain lion.

Vibrant with expectancy, Nate slowly raised the Hawken to his shoulder. It suddenly occurred to him that he had a clear shot in front of his hiding place but the brush obstructed his view to either side. Should Satan charge from those directions he would have virtually no time to react. You idiot! he reflected. Why didn't you think of that sooner?

Behind Nate the stallion and two other mares added their nickers to those of the decoy. The horses were making so much noise Nate wouldn't be able to hear the panther cross the stream. Annoyed, he twisted to shush them, or started to, when his startled eyes fell on Old Satan. The monster wasn't more than ten feet off to the west, crouched belly to the ground, its long snakelike tail twitching madly as it glanced from the unsuspecting decoy to the horses by the dwindling fire and back again.

Nate was flabbergasted. He'd had no inkling the panther was so close. Evidently the mare was gazing at something else, or the panther had moved upstream and crossed without the mare seeing it. In order to shoot he would have to rise to his knees and swing around, giving the panther all the forewarning needed to bound off unscathed. Should he try anyway? Indecisive, he held himself rigid, waiting to see if the cat would move closer.

Satan appeared equally indecisive, continuing to divide his attention between the decoy and the other horses. At length the panther concentrated solely on the lone mare and crept toward her, claws extended.

Nate held his breath. Once the cat came near enough, it would be all over. As quick as panthers were, they couldn't evade a shot at point-blank rage. He counted down the feet and girded himself to spring from hiding. Eight feet. Six feet.

At the very moment Nate was about to leap up, Satan halted and looked directly at the brush. Directly at *him*. Nate could practically feel the panther's infernal eyes boring into his, and he couldn't repress a slight shudder at a mental picture of the cat leaping on him before he could stand and rending him limb from limb. He'd be pinned down, helpless to resist.

Nate had no idea whether the panther knew he was there or whether it was merely suspicious. Had the beast heard him? He hadn't moved since spying it. Had his scent given him away? Not likely, since the wind was blowing toward him. What, then?

Satan abruptly uttered a low growl that carried to Nate's ears alone; as yet, the decoy was unaware of the predator's presence. Muscles working like coiled steel springs, the cat inched its right leg forward, then its left. But instead of creeping toward the decoy, it came straight toward the depression!

Nate was in a dire predicament. So long as the element of surprise had been in his favor, he had an edge. His advantage gone, there was only one option. He must jump up and shoot. Unfortunately, doing so would hasten the cat's attack. And he held no illusions about which one of them was the fastest.

The stallion voiced a challenge that prompted the panther to stop and glare. Nate heard his horse stomp its forefeet, saw Satan hiss and turn a few degrees toward the fire. That was all the opening he needed. Surging from concealment, he trained the Hawken on the cat's ribs, cocked the hammer, and tapped the trigger. Swift as he was, he couldn't compare to the panther.

As the brush burst upward, Satan whirled and flashed toward the spruce trees, clearing twenty feet at a leap. In the middle of the cat's second leap, Nate fired, his slug missing by a hair and thudding into the dirt under the panther's hindquarters. Satan's speed didn't allow for a second shot.

The undergrowth closed on the lion as Nate snatched at his powder horn and rapidly reloaded. Although his twin pistols were heavy-caliber, he'd rather have the sheer stopping power of the Hawken at his disposal. Precious seconds were lost as he fed powder, ball, and blanket wad down the barrel. Then, although he stood no chance of overtaking Satan, he raced into the trees, slanting toward the stream as the cat had done. Maybe, just maybe, he'd get at least one more shot.

Nate broke from cover near the water and squatted. Disappointment racked him on discovering the lion had effected its escape. He smacked his leg in anger, then stiffened as the night was torn by a ferocious snarl—*coming from the camp!* Satan had used the same ruse as last time, circling around while he chased shadows!

Witnesses would have been dazzled by Nate's fleetness of foot. Panicked whinnies mingled with raspy growls spurred him to his peak, and he weaved among the pines with abandon born of desperation. The horses were being set upon, the stallion and the mares by the fire, and from the sound of things they were in grave peril.

A single tree blocked the clearing when a strident neigh foretold a stricken horse. Nate's blood turned chill. He gained the camp and saw the panther clinging to the haunches of one of the mares, its wicked claws gouging deep furrows in her buttocks, thighs, and flanks. He took a stride to obtain a better angle and the mountain lion, which hadn't been looking in his direction but seemed somehow to sense his presence, sprang to the ground and fairly skimmed the grass as it fled.

"Not this time!" Nate shouted, swinging the rifle to compensate. He stroked the trigger, felt the stock smack into his shoulder. The panther jerked to one side, nearly fell, recovered, and gained the brush with a prodigious leap.

Nate yanked out a flintlock and ran to the thicket. He longed to see the cat convulsing in the bushes, but he should have known better. Satan was gone. There wasn't so much as a broken branch to show which way the lion had headed.

Turning, Nate dashed to the hurt mare. The fire had died to flickering fingers of flame so he added several pieces of dry wood. In the flare of light the deep cuts resembled a welter of scarlet ribbons. Blood flowed down the mare's rear legs and formed a spreading pool under her tail. Wincing in sympathy for the agony the horse was enduring, Nate set down his rifle and collected handfuls of grass which he used in an attempt to stanch the flow. Throughout, the mare stood as docile as a lamb, head bowed, saliva drooling from her chin.

The grass slowed the bleeding but didn't stop it, compelling Nate to resort to a crude remedy he'd once seen a Shoshone warrior employ. The Shoshone had been on a buffalo surround during which his favorite war horse had been gored in the stomach by an enraged bull. In a bid to save the prized mount from certain death, the warrior applied regular mud packs to the holes. Nate had secretly doubted the treatment would be of any benefit, yet to his amazement the horse recovered.

There was plenty of mud along the stream. Nate made eight trips, carrying as much as he could hold without getting it all over himself. The mare fidgeted when he applied a thick, dank layer, as he might the frosting on a cake, into the furrows the panther had torn from her flesh. When he was done, Nate stroked the mare's neck and stared over her shoulders at the benighted woodland. "I'll get you yet, you bastard," he declared grimly. "Wait and see."

As if in defiant answer, from the vicinity of a mountain half a mile to the south wafted the shrill shriek of Old Satan.

Chapter Five

"I'll get you. Just wait and see."

The boy squatted next to the mouse hole and hefted the club taken from the wood box. He had to use two hands to swing it with any force. Leaning back against the wall, he stared at the piece of cheese lying a yard away. Sooner or later the mouse would come out after the morsel and the boy would do as his father wanted and bash the creature's brains in. The very thought made the boy's stomach churn but he fought the sensation. He had to do as his father told him. He had to prove he wasn't an idler and worthless dreamer as his father believed.

The boy wanted his father to be proud of him. If he killed the mouse, maybe his father would stop being so critical. Of late they spent all their time arguing, a situation that got worse the older the boy became. He didn't understand why. When he had been younger, he'd gotten along wonderfully with both his parents. Now he was always being criticized, always being labelled as lazy and worthless. Yet he was the same person he had always been, and he never griped about doing his fair share of the chores. So why was his father forever carping about every little thing he did?

Troubled, the boy looked up as a shadow fell across the floor. He beamed in delight at the woman who entered the kitchen and said softly, "You won't have to worry about this mouse much longer, Mother."

She paused, blinked at seeing him, and frowned at the hole. "So your father picked you, did he?"

An edge to her tone prompted the boy to ask, "Is something wrong?"

The mother's face clouded and she gripped her dress so tight her knuckles turned white. "No, son. Everything is just fine. You be sure and do as your father tells you."

"He said the mouse gave you a bad scare."

"Did he indeed?" She averted her gaze. "Well, if your father said it, it must be true."

"I can't believe a little mouse would bother you. You're too"—the boy paused, seeking the right word, and chose—"mature."

He was greatly startled when his mother unexpectedly turned, came quickly over, and gave him a hug that threatened to bust his ribs. When she stepped back, she spun around before he could see her features.

"Are you all right?"

"I'm fine, son," she said, her voice rather husky.

"You sure?"

"Of course. Now stay quiet so the mouse will come out." Off she went, her head bowed.

The boy was puzzled by her strange behavior. There had been a time when his mother had been full of life and laughter and being around her had made him all warm inside. Now she upset him terribly because she was always so moody. Yet she had no reason to be. Grown-ups were impossible to figure out.

The boy wagged the bludgeon, concentrated on the hole, and waited.

The next morning dawned grey and somber with a promise of moisture in the rarified air. Nate was no sooner out of the blankets than he checked on the mare. She was dozing and only cracked an eye when he gently touched her. Her hind quarters were terribly swollen but thankfully the bleeding had stopped. Nate replaced the dry mud with a new layer. Then, and only then, did he warm his stomach with four cups of steaming coffee. Usually his morning brew perked him up. Not today. Circumstances forced him to make a decision he would rather not have to make.

The mare was too weak to go anywhere. Nate either left her in camp while he made his rounds of the traps, which would leave her at the mercy of Satan should the panther show up, or he stayed in camp until the mare was strong enough to tag along. That would take days, though. And during that time the mountain lion would wreak vengeance on any beaver caught in the traps, destroying their pelts.

Nate quaffed the last of his fourth cup, then set the cup on a flat rock beside the fire. No matter what he decided, he stood to lose. Which did he value more? The mare or the hides? The horse had been loyal and had never given him cause to complain, but by the same token he couldn't very well stand by and do nothing while the hellish cat made mincemeat of the beaver. He was damned if he did, damned if he didn't.

The sky gradually brightened although the sun was

unable to put in an appearance thanks to the growing cloud cover. Nate made no move to mount up. Twice he examined the mare. At length he voiced a string of oaths and prepared to leave. He hesitated with a foot in a stirrup, glanced at the fire, and had a brainstorm.

It took twenty minutes to gather enough wood for four more fires, arranged in a ring around the suffering horse. To each he added enough fuel to last an hour, minimum. "This is the best I can do," he told the mare. "Cats are afraid of fire. Maybe this will keep Satan at bay until I get back."

Then Nate climbed onto the stallion and rode off with the two other pack animals in tow. He intended to hurry, but along a northern tributary he found five beaver and up another he found three, the most caught at any one time since his arrival. Each had to be retrieved, the traps reset and placed elsewhere. Several hours elapsed. By his reckoning the time was close to noon when he caught sight of the camp. And something else.

A large, ungainly black bird was gliding down toward the clearing, pinions spread wide to soar on the currents, its reddish head cocked to one side.

Nate took one look and prodded the stallion into a gallop. As he clattered past the thicket he discovered five more buzzards either perched on the mare or next to her. Several had strips of bloody flesh hanging from their breaks. Some hissed on seeing Nate appear. As he bore down on them they hopped into the air and flapped frantically, fleeing every which way.

Nate paid them no heed. He vaulted from the saddle and dashed to the mare. Feeling for a heartbeat wasn't necessary. She had been dead for some time, her throat slashed wide open, her jugular severed. A pool of blood was soaking into the soil. Other claw marks were on her neck and head. Portions of her side had been torn out in bite-sized chunks.

"Satan!" Nate stated harshly, his fists clenched. A survey of the clearing turned up three partial prints, enough to tell the story.

The mare had most probably been asleep, the fires long out, when the panther sprang out of the spruce trees and in a few mighty bounds pounced on her neck. Two or three swipes of its razor claws had been enough to rip her throat apart. Then the cat had slashed and bit its prey numerous times in savage glee.

Her death bothered Nate. He tried telling himself it shouldn't, that such incidents were commonplace in the Rockies. Violence and dying were an integral part of Nature. Each and every day countless animals fell victim to hungry meat eaters. Nate knew he should be accustomed to the endless cycle of killing by now, but this was different. The mare had been a companion of sorts, not just another wild beast.

And, too, Nate was incensed at Satan. The wily lion had outmaneuvered him—again. Was it out there right this minute, observing his every move? He searched the vegetation without success.

A pressing problem presented itself. The mare was too big to bury. Nor could the carcass be left there to rot, not if Nate intended to call the clearing home until it was time to rejoin Shakespeare. Finding a new spot to camp, moving all the supplies and pelts, and erecting another lean-to would cost him another day or two. Since he wasn't too fond of the idea of staying in that valley a minute longer than necessary, he had to think of a means of moving the mare.

Nate selected the thickest limb he could carry, wedged an end under the mare, and tried flipping her body over.

The limb snapped like kindling. Relying on a lever proved a waste of energy.

Undaunted, Nate walked to his packs and found the long coil of rope he invariably brought along. Getting the rope around the mare's body took considerable effort and ingenuity and left blood smeared on his leggings and moccasins, prompting a trip to the stream to wash up. Then he mounted the stallion and tried hauling the mare off, but although the obedient black strained and tugged and heaved, the weight was too much for any one horse to move.

"I'm not licked yet," Nate declared, swinging down. Drawing his butcher knife, he sliced the rope in half, giving him two. One end of the severed length was tied to the mare, the other end around the neck of one of the remaining pack animals. Grasping the stallion's reins and the pack animal's lead, Nate guided them toward the thicket to the south. When the ropes lost all slack and both horses stopped, he gave a pull and urged them on with shouts of encouragement. Gradually, inch by laboriously gained inch, the mare's body was moved.

The job took nearly two hours. Nate was afraid the ropes would break so whenever they seemed on the verge of splitting he rested the stallion and pack horse a few minutes. In this manner he was able to drag the mare a distance of forty yards.

Untying the ropes, Nate rode back and rekindled the fire. He spent the afternoon skinning beaver and working on their hides. With the red sun hovering above the stark western peaks, he made his customary circuit of the traps and was mildly disappointed to end up empty-handed.

"Maybe I should leave early," Nate said to the stallion. "Maybe there aren't as many beaver left as I thought." He'd developed the habit of talking to the big black as if it was his best friend, and the stallion accommodated by pricking its ears whenever he spoke. "I've got enough as it is, anyway. Why be greedy?"

No buzzards swooped over the clearing this time, but there was something far worse. Nate rounded a spruce tree and drew rein in consternation, his face flushing beet red. "What the hell!" he roared. "I'll nail that panther's hide to my cabin wall!"

Old Satan had paid the camp a visit in Nate's absence. The mountain lion had scattered parfleches and packs all over, tearing many open. Worse, a small bale of plews, representing two full weeks of work, was missing.

Nate was fit to be tied. He stormed about the clearing hunting for tracks. Finding none, he insured the Hawken was loaded and hiked in ever widening circles around the camp, determined to find the missing bale before darkness set in. Time worked against him. So did his own common sense when he realized he had left the horses unattended. Reluctantly, he gave up after only a few minutes.

A magnificent full moon adorned the heavens but Nate wasn't in any frame of mind to appreciate the celestial spectacle. He sipped coffee and mulled what he should do next. Obviously the panther had it in for him. Perhaps Satan regarded the valley as its exclusive domain. Whatever the reason, the cat had to be the most spiteful beast alive, and it was as plain as the nose on Nate's face that it would continue to torment him until he departed.

Running went against Nate's grain, yet what else could he do? The loss of another horse or bale would be disastrous. Better to cut his losses while he could. Later on maybe he would return with a few Shoshone friends and settle accounts.

Nate slept fitfully that night. Up before daylight, he hid the rest of his bales in the spruce trees, using the ropes to hoist them high onto sturdy branches. Convinced the plews were safe, he secreted his packs in the depression he had dug near the stream, then covered them with brush.

"That ought to do it," Nate announced. Forgoing coffee, he climbed on the stallion and started collecting the Newhouses. At midday he brought those he had gathered to the clearing and immediately rode out after more. By late in the day he had reclaimed two-thirds of the traps. He could have collected another half-dozen or so, but he still wanted to scour the area around his camp for the missing bale.

Tethering the pack animals in the very center of the clearing where they would be able to see the panther if it came at them and whinny in alarm, Nate, acting on a hunch, rode the stallion into the spruce trees. The bale weighed upwards of fifty pounds and would be hard to drag off, even for Old Satan. The thickets were too dense for the cat to make much headway, and Nate couldn't see the lion lugging the bale across the stream. Making the spruce trees the best bet.

The guess turned out to be accurate. Beyond the spruce trees lay a meadow. Nate gazed out over it and saw brown spots among the high grass. Applying his heels, he galloped to the nearest one, his anger surging at the sight of a pelt that had been torn into ragged sections. It was the same with the next hide, and the next. Satan had used teeth and claws to rend the plews asunder.

Not once in Nate's entire life had he heard of a panther doing such a thing. He made a sweep of the entire meadow and discovered only three hides intact. These he took with him.

Mountain Cat

The prospect of another night in the valley was mildly unnerving. Nate was actually anxious to leave, but he had the remainder of the traps to bring in. Provided that luck smiled on him, he'd be ready to go by noon of the next day at the very latest.

As an added precaution, Nate tore out bushes by the roots and piled them in a waist-high circle in the clearing. The barrier didn't offer much protection, but the panther would be unable to get at the horses and him without leaping over it. And if he had to, he could set the barrier alight to drive the cat off.

Nate ate glumly, wolfing beaver meat without relish. Afterward he sat up sipping coffee until well past midnight. To his surprise, Satan didn't appear, nor did the valley echo to the lion's throaty snarls. Propped against his saddle, he fell asleep with a pistol in each hand.

A whinny awakened Nate hours later. By the positions of the stars and constellations he knew the time was about four in the morning. All three horses were excited by something south of the barrier. Rising and stepping to the stallion, he gripped its mane and quietly straddled its broad back. From his vantage point he commanded a sweeping view of the clearing.

Satan was so close to the barrier Nate could have hit the cat with a stone. In the pale moonlight its coat had a whitish sheen. The lion appeared baffled by the wall of brush and was silently pacing back and forth.

Nate extended both flintlocks slowly so as not to draw attention to himself. He aimed carefully at the panther's head and curled his thumbs around the hammers. They would click when cocked, which couldn't be helped. The worst that might happen was the monster would run off. If not, the smoothbore .55-caliber pistols would end Satan's career then and there.

Grinning in anticipation, Nate jerked the hammers back. They did indeed click, loudly, too, and the panther reacted accordingly before Nate could fire. However, not in the fashion Nate expected. Instead of racing off, the mountain lion whirled, took a single leap, and cleared the top of the brush barrier with feet to spare, springing straight at Nate.

In the blink of an eye Nate compensated, training both pistols on the hurtling cat, but as he did the black stallion reared and he had to clutch at the stallion's mane to keep from being thrown off. In the act of rearing, the stallion pulled free of its tether.

Satan alighted in front of the stallion and raked the horse with its claws, then evaded a flurry of pounding hoofs. Nate raised one arm to fire. Again he was thwarted when the stallion abruptly leaped and sailed over the brush. Nate tried to stop the horse before it reached the thicket but the stallion ignored the pressure of his legs and arms.

"Whoa!" Nate shouted frantically. "Whoa, big fellow!" He jammed the flintlocks under his belt to free his hands so he could grab at the rope dangling from the stallion's neck. Bending forward, he snatched it and straightened just as the black burst from the thicket and entered the forest.

Nate looked up, saw a low tree limb sweeping at his face, and ducked. The limb struck his beaver hat sending it flying. He glanced back, wanting to note the exact spot so he could come back later, but the dark shadows made the area a murky soup.

"Stop, damn it!" Nate thundered, hauling on the rope with all his strength. The stallion, fired with fear, sped onward into the night.

Nate tried not to think of what might be happening

to his mares. Repeatedly he tried to halt the stallion. When it wouldn't obey, he tensed, preparing to leap off and run to the clearing to prevent the mountain lion from slaughtering the pack horses, if it hadn't already done so.

Bracing both hands on the stallion's back, Nate shoved upward. Too late he glimpsed another limb rushing toward him. He threw up his arms to protect himself. The limb smashed him in the temple. Excrutiating pain racked him from head to toe and he was catapulted end over end. Dimly he was aware of crashing down, of the drum of the stallion's hoofs rapidly receding.

Then all went black.

Somewhere else. Long ago.

The boy felt a hand on his shoulder and his eyes snapped wide with fright. He stared into the hard features of his father and inwardly struggled to calm himself.

"Is this how you do a job I ask you to do? You fall asleep?"

"I'm sorry, Father. It's been hours and the mouse hasn't shown itself."

"Oh?" The father pivoted, pointed at the cheese. It had been gnawed clean through and half of it was missing. "See those little teeth marks? What do you think the mouse was doing while you were being your usual lazy self?"

"I didn't hear it!" the boy blurted.

"That's your excuse? The mouse should have been polite enough to make more noise so you could wake up and kill it?"

"I didn't say—" the boy began, and recoiled when he was cuffed on the ear.

"What have I told you about sassing me, son?" the

father demanded in a strained tone. "Haven't I told you again and again never to talk back to your mother or me?"

"Yes."

"Yes, what?"

"Yes, sir."

A protracted sigh issued from the father and he slowly stood. "What am I going to do with you? I try and try to teach you how to be behave. I do my best to show you what it takes to be successful in this vicious world of ours. But you won't pay me any mind." He sadly shook his head. "I've never known anyone so lazy in all my days."

An angry retort reached the boy's lips but went no further. His ear still stung terribly.

"I know what you're thinking," the father declared. "It's just a tiny mouse. Why am I making such an issue of it?" He nudged the cheese with a toe. "There must be some way of impressing the point I'm trying to make."

"I won't fall asleep again. I promise," the boy said.

"You'd better not or I'll tan your backside," the father warned. "You're not too old for a switching." Turning, he took a few paces, then drew up short and snapped his fingers. "Of course! I saw him just a few minutes ago on my way home! Drop that piece of wood and come with me."

"Where are we going?"

"Don't ask questions," the father barked. Grabbing the boy by the shirt, he hurried to the front door. The sidewalk was packed with people, while in the street a steady stream of creaking carriages and rattling wagons flowed to and fro.

The boy was hustled two blocks to an intersection

with a main avenue. Here there were many more people, many more carriages. His father stopped in the midst of the bedlam and grinned. The boy looked all around in confusion, afraid to ask a question for fear of being ridiculed.

"See him, son?"

"Who, father?"

"One Leg, of course. Over by that wall."

The beggar had a name but no one knew it so everyone in the neighborhood called him One Leg. He was ancient, with wrinkles in his wrinkles, his clothes little more than grimy rags. Every day of the week except the Lord's day he could be found on this particular corner, battered tin cup on the ground in front of him to receive whatever alms were offered.

"Do you understand now?" the father asked.

No, the boy didn't. So he hesitated, uncertain of the right answer, and his father went on excitedly.

"This is what comes of being lazy, son. This is why I try to instill in you a dedication to hard work and discipline. I don't want you to end your days like One Leg." The father's voice dripped contempt. "He doesn't have to make a living this way. There are jobs he could do if he really wanted to. But all he does is sit on his backside, depending on the kindness of strangers for his livelihood. Do you want to be like him?"

"No," the boy said. In his heart he was deeply sorry for anyone who had to suffer so much.

"Good. I'm delighted you finally see the light. Now let's go home so you can kill that mouse. And if you start to doze off again, you just think of One Leg. That should set you straight."

"Yes, sir," the boy agreed, although truth to tell he was at a loss to see how his father could compare the beggar's pathetic plight to killing a lowly rodent. After all, One Leg hadn't asked to lose a limb.

"One day you'll thank me for this lesson," the father said proudly.

"I'm sure I will."

Chapter Six

Warm sunshine tingling Nate King's face returned him to the land of the living. He sat up with a start and immediately regretted doing so when a tremendous bolt of anguish shot through him. Groaning, he placed a hand on his temple and felt his palm grow sticky with half-dried blood. He flinched as he probed gently with his fingertips, tracing the outline of a ragged gash.

Propping a hand under him, Nate pushed to his feet, swayed at an onslaught of dizziness, and would have fallen had he not reached out and leaned against a tree. By the height of the sun he guessed he'd been unconscious for four or five hours. He scanned the woods for the stallion but saw only chipmunks.

"Damn," Nate muttered. For all he knew, the black was halfway to Shoshone country. He would have to rely on one of the mares. At the thought he stiffened. Then he shuffled toward the camp, drawing both pistols when the thicket came in sight. He feared the worst, and his fears were realized.

Part of the brush barrier had been destroyed, barreled aside by a terrified pack animal. Drops of blood showed the mare had been hurt, and also showed she had fled eastward. The second horse hadn't been so lucky.

Satan had brought the animal down by severing the tendons on her rear legs. Once the mare had been hamstrung, the panther had finished her off at his leisure, clawing great chunks from her body, slicing her neck to ribbons, and taking bites from various spots. The horse had died awash in a thick bath of her blood, and what remained was coated with crimson.

Not content with slaying the pack animal, Satan had turned his wrath on Nate's belongings. The saddle bore a dozen claw cuts. The blankets had been frayed. A parfleche had been reduced to scrap leather. Not a single item was worth being salvaged.

Where was the Hawken? Nate wondered in dismay. He needed the rifle if he was to have any hope of escaping the valley alive. A search of the bloody area inside the barrier was fruitless. He expanded his search to the clearing with the same result. Pulse quickening, he hunted among the spruce trees. Persistence kept him at it for half an hour, at which point thirst took him to the stream. He was kneeling to dip his hands in the crystal clear water when he saw his rifle lying nearby. Grinning, he dashed over and scooped it up. Other than teeth marks on the stock, the rifle was undamaged.

Renewed confidence invigorated Nate. He drank heartily, then washed his wound, gritting his teeth against the torment. Going to the depression, he removed some of the brush and withdrew a parfleche containing jerky and pemmican. This went over his left shoulder.

He rummaged in a pack for an old blanket he kept on hand as a spare. From this he cut a wide strip, dabbed the strip in the stream, and wrapped it once about his head, securing it with a knot at the back.

Nate was almost ready. The rest of the bales were safe in the trees. The rest of his provisions were hidden in the depression. The traps he placed deep in a thicket where the rain couldn't get at them. Then Nate hiked eastward, staying close to the stream where the going was easy. He chewed on jerky and kept alert for sign of Old Satan. All he wanted was one good shot, one chance to pay the monster back for the pain and all he had lost. Remaining in the valley would be foolish. Nate planned to head south and find McNair. The two of them would come back for his things, get in and out in a single day in order to avoid the panther. It was the best he could do under the circumstances. He should be thankful that he had enough pelts left to bring in a tidy sum at the rendezvous.

Nate recalled how his heart had leaped into his throat when the panther leaped at him the night before, and he marveled yet once more at the cat's actions. Such relentless conduct was so extraordinary he doubted anyone would believe him when he told the tale. If he told the story. It embarrassed him to think he had been beaten by a wild beast. He'd long believed that with a little hard work and discipline a person could surmount any problem, could overcome any hardship. Yet here he'd been put to the test and found wanting.

Hours later Nate came abreast of the hill he had descended to enter the valley. Scaling it on foot was an arduous labor. He often had to pause to rest. On reaching the crest he turned and gazed down on Satan's shaded valley, and in an act of sheer spite he cupped a hand to his mouth and voiced a series of Shoshone war whoops. They echoed off the mountains, rolling out across the valley in both directions. Wherever Satan was, he was bound to hear them.

Chuckling, Nate squared his shoulders and resumed trekking southward. Despite the nightmare, he was in fine spirits. He had food, he had ammunition. He had his rifle, pistols, knife, and tomahawk. He could live off the land almost as well as any Indian. In short, he was supremely confident he would reach his friend within a few days and his ordeal would be over.

The wildlife afforded ample entertainment. Whether it was squirrels scampering in the trees or ravens winging overhead or deer spooked from cover, there was always something happening. Once Nate spied moving brown spots on steep cliffs to the west. Bighorns, they were, bounding along the cliff face with unmatched ease, as unaffected by the dizzying heights below as if they were on solid ground.

Later, Nate spotted a small herd of shaggy mountain buffalo. He stopped, lifted the Hawken, then changed his mind. It had been ages since he ate a juicy steak, and merely looking at the grazing brutes made his mouth water, his stomach rumble. But he couldn't eat a whole buffalo at one sitting and he didn't have the means of packing the excess out. So rather than waste so much meat, he continued walking.

The sun arced westward, lengthening the shadows. Nate nibbled on jerky and looked for a spot to camp for the night. His head was torturing him. He'd turn in early, enjoy a decent sleep, and be full of vigor and vim come daylight.

A hare provided Nate's supper. Lacking a pot to cook stew, he chopped the meat into square bits, then skewered them on a sharpened stick and held them over the fire until they were done. He ate with relish, wiping his greasy fingers on his leggings. For a bed he spread pine needles and grass to form a mat an inch thick.

That night Nate slept better than he had in days. Leftover hare was his breakfast. As the sun peeked above the horizon, he adjusted his possibles bag and ammunition pouch, shouldered the spare parfleche, and headed out.

Nate whistled as he walked, his rifle balanced across his left shoulder. The more distance he put between himself and the valley, the happier he felt. His previous worries seemed downright silly, and he convinced himself that he had let his imagination get the better of him by exaggerating Satan's prowess. Toward the end there he had regarded the panther as if it had been a demon instead of just another oversized cat. True, it had an incredibly savage temperament. But Satan was a run-of-the-mill panther, nothing more.

Noon found Nate at a creek. Upon slaking his thirst he removed his bandage and washed the wound. It was healing nicely and gave no indication of being infected. He stripped off his buckskins and sat in a small pool splashing cool water on his chest and back. Refreshed, he followed the creek for over a mile, until it angled eastward and he had to journey on to the south.

Nate had hoped he would reach Shakespeare's valley before the second day was up, but since he was making a beeline for the valley instead of taking the easiest route as he had on the stallion, the exceptionally rugged terrain slowed him down. Deadfalls, ravines, and cliffs all had to be skirted or negotiated with extreme caution. Consequently he was several miles from his destination when twilight claimed the mountains.

Nate's sleep was even more restful than it had been the first night. He had chosen a sheltered spot close to the bottom of a towering cliff, as he had once before. At dawn he was up, eager to go on. Taking a piece of pemmican from the parfleche, he bit down and started walking, absently gazing at the cliff above. A patch of brown against the background of solid rock arrested his attention and he stared at it to see if it would move, certain it was another bighorn. Seconds later the creature rose off its haunches and walked a few yards, and when it did, Nate's mouth went slack and the pemmican fell to the grass.

The animal wasn't a bighorn at all.

It was Satan.

Long ago. Far away.

The boy was growing drowsy again. To keep from falling asleep and arousing his father's anger, he stared out the kitchen window at the big oak tree in the back yard. A robin sat on a branch chirping its little heart out. The boy smiled, envying the bird its lust for life. And its freedom. The robin could go where it wanted, when it wanted. It never had anyone telling it what to do or how to live its life. How the boy wished he might have the same sort of freedom!

Motion registered at the corner of the boy's eye and he swung his head around. Although he should have expected to see what he saw, he was nonetheless stunned to behold a mouse nibbling on the cheese. A tiny, harmless rodent with big, appealing eyes, its whiskers twitching as its mouth worked in a hungry frenzy.

The boy was mesmerized. He gawked in fascination, completely forgetting about the club in his hands. Never had he seen mice close up before. He hadn't realized how very teeny they were, how delicate they appeared. The thought of crushing this one to a pulp caused his tummy to flutter.

A distant sound made the mouse suddenly stop eating and raise its head high to sniff the air. When assured there was no threat, it bit into the cheese with renewed enthusiasm.

Reluctantly the boy firmed his grip on the club. He had a job to do, whether he liked doing it or not. As his parents had pointed out, where there was one mouse, there were always more, and if left to breed uncontrolled they could infest a house from cellar to attic. Worse, they sometimes carried diseases. So the rodent had to be exterminated for the good of his family.

But the boy hesitated, unable to bring himself to perform the deed. The mouse was so fragile looking, so innocent. How could he kill it?

Over a minute went by and the dainty creature polished off most of the cheese. The boy had to do something soon or it would scurry into the hole. Girding himself, he raised the wood over his head, but he did so slowly, not with the speed required to strike in time to stop the mouse from escaping. The rodent predictably whirled and scurried into its sanctuary. Rather than being upset, the boy grinned.

"What do you think you are doing?"

Shocked, the boy looked up to find his father framed in the doorway. "I tried to kill the mouse," he blurted even though he knew better.

"If there's one thing I can't stand, it's a liar," the father said gruffly, advancing and cuffing the boy on the head so hard the boy was knocked onto his backside. "I just stood there and saw you deliberately let that mouse get away. Why? What in the world were you thinking of?"

David Thompson

The boy rubbed his ear and clenched his teeth.

"Two days now you've been at this and you haven't killed a single mouse," the father criticized. "When I was your age, I would have had six or seven squashed by now. What excuse do you have?"

"None," the boy confessed.

"No, you don't. And frankly, I'm tired of this nonsense." The father went to the cupboard and obtained another small piece of cheese. "Listen to me, young man," he declared. "You're going to do as I want whether you like it or not. I won't have a shirker in my family. When there's work to be done, we do it."

"Yes, sir."

The father deposited the cheese at the same place on the floor. "I want you to know that if it was up to me, I'd use poison. But your mother is afraid her darling dog would get hold of some. So we have to do this the hard way." He glanced at the mouse hole. "You might be wondering why I don't go out and buy one of the traps available. Why should I waste the money when you can do the job just as well or better?"

"You have always taught us to be thrifty, Father."

"Take my advice. The sooner you get this done, the sooner you can go waste your time reading." The father walked to the door, then looked over his shoulder. "Sometimes we have to do things we don't like doing, son. We have to take the bad with the good, as it were."

"I know."

"Do you? I wonder." The father frowned. "If you learn nothing else from this experience, learn this. The bad things in our life just don't up and vanish because we want them to go away. We have to face problems head on and overcome them or they'll keep coming back to haunt us later."

Mountain Cat

*   *   *

Nate King gaped at the monster cat in disbelief. A wave of apprehension washed over him and there was a sinking sensation in his gut. It couldn't be! And yet there the panther sat, gazing down at him from its lofty roost! The damn beast had trailed him all the way from the valley, had no doubt been shadowing him all along. Why? What did it have in mind?

The answer was obvious. Satan had no intention of allowing him to get away. The panther was stalking him, biding its time until it could take him unawares. The hunter had become the hunted.

But the very notion was preposterous! Nate reflected. Panthers didn't track down people as they would other game. Quite the contrary. Panthers went out of their way to avoid human beings. Or most did, anyway, because there was no denying the testimony of his own eyes.

Nate raised the Hawken, realized he would be wasting the lead ball, and jerked the rifle down again. What should he do? Go up after the cat? No. Attempting to climb the cliff would be certain suicide.

Cradling the rifle in the crook of an elbow, Nate marched southward. Perhaps he was becoming over-wrought for no reason. The panther hadn't attacked him since he left the valley, had it? And before nightfall he would be back with Shakespeare, wouldn't he? If the cat showed itself then, the two of them would ride it down, and whoever shot it would have a glorious trophy to mount on the wall of his cabin.

At the edge of the pines Nate glanced up. The mountain lion was gone. He raised a hand to shield his eyes from the bright sunlight reflected off the cliff face and scanned the rim to where it sloped down into the forest a quarter of a mile ahead. There was a chance he could ambush the panther if he could get there before the cat did.

Nate ran for all he was worth. Satan had outsmarted himself by taking to the high ground. There was just the one way down, since not even a mountain lion could descend a sheer rock wall. Nate would soon have the predator right in his sights!

Only someone with iron sinews and superbly conditioned to the high altitude could have reached the side of the cliff in so short a time. Crouching behind a boulder, Nate scoured the slope. Satan was bound to appear at any moment. He cocked the Hawken, rested the barrel on top of the boulder, and smirked. I'm ready for you, you hoodoo killer! he thought. Come and be rubbed out!

By all rights the panther should have appeared. Minutes dragged by and it didn't. Perplexed, Nate climbed on top of the boulder to see if he could spot the tawny shape somewhere above. Either Satan was hiding or the cat had gone the other way.

On a spur of the moment decision, Nate ran up the slope to the rim. He couldn't let this golden opportunity pass. The panther wouldn't be expecting him to go after it, so he'd have an edge. Stealthily working his way along the narrow shelf that crowned the cliff, he held his finger lightly on the trigger.

To say Nate was upset when he had gone over fifty yards and not found his quarry was an understatement. He stopped, ascended a jumbled pile of boulders to the uppermost slab, and surveyed the shelf before him. It was as if the ground had opened up and swallowed the panther whole.

Just then, in the forest at the bottom of the south slope, a mountain lion coughed.

Nate swung around and glowered in exasperation.

Mountain Cat

Somehow, Satan had gotten to the woods before he got to the slope. All the time he had been looking for the cat at the top of the cliff, the cat had been resting in the shade of the evergreens. It was enough to make him want to hit something, so he did, slapping the slab and stinging his palm.

Retracing his steps, Nate was presently among the pines again. He figured Satan was ahead of him, and he searched diligently for tracks. The cat was too clever for him. All he located was a partial print that might or might not be that of a panther.

As Nate straightened he noticed the wildlife had fallen totally silent as it had that day he'd been en route to the dark valley, leading him to speculate on whether Satan had been stalking him far longer than he supposed. It was a disturbing feeling to find oneself the prey of one of the most fierce carnivores inhabiting the Rockies. Now he knew how a deer or an elk felt under similar circumstances.

Except there was an important difference. Unlike a deer or an elk, Nate could easily slay the big cat if he could only get a shot at it. To this end he vigilantly advanced. The eerie stillness rasped on his nerves, and he was almost grateful when a squirrel commenced raising a racket off to the right. Then it occurred to him that the cause of the squirrel's outrage might be the mountain lion.

Changing direction, Nate went from cover to cover until he spied the chattering denizen of the upper terraces high on the limb of a fir tree. The squirrel was staring at undergrowth a score of yards from the trunk. Flattening, Nate studied the wall of vegetation. He was certain Satan was in there, and equally certain there must a method of luring the cat out.

A rock suggested a means. Nate picked it up, hefted it a few times, then hurled the rock as far as he could to the left. It hit in a tree and clattered off a number of branches before thudding to earth.

A patch of underbrush moved.

Nate sighted on the spot and held the Hawken steady. As soon as the panther showed its hairy face, he'd core its brain with a lead ball. He waited, and waited. The squirrel kept on chattering. The breeze increased, swaying the branches overhead. And the panther failed to materialize.

Again Nate tried to entice the lion into the open by tossing a rock, this time close to the underbrush where Satan was concealed. Not so much as a twig stirred. Puzzled, Nate crawled forward, setting his elbows and knees down gently to muffle the noise.

Every mountain man knew that it was easier to see a moving object when low to the ground. An erect man might miss spying a moving buck in a thicket because the color of the buck's hide blended so well into the background. The same man, if crouched or lying down, would be more apt to detect the difference because the angle reduced the effect of the background.

So Nate remained flat on his stomach, and when he came to the undergrowth he snaked into its depths rather than stand and walk. A pungent odor stopped him. He didn't have to look hard for the source, a pile of raccoon droppings by his elbow, droppings so fresh they were runny.

Was that what the squirrel had seen? Nate mused. A raccoon? Avoiding the pile, he wound farther into the recesses of the brushwood. Suddenly, a flurry of activity erupted thirty feet distant. There was some sort of struggle going on. Nate lurched into a run, stooping to pass under scrub trees. He saw a tawny form and another, smaller shape, swirling around one another.

Nate was almost upon them when the tawny creature sped to the northwest. The outline of the panther was unmistakable and he couldn't resist dropping to one knee, aiming, and firing. Whether his shot was on the mark or not was impossible to tell. Apparently not, since Satan faded into the greenery without slowing the slightest bit.

Reloading on the run, Nate came to where the commotion had been and found a large male raccoon lying on its side, its lifeblood gushing from a ruptured throat, its intestines spilling from a ruptured belly. The panther had attacked it but not bothered to carry it off to eat. Wanton slaughter was all the beast seemed to live for.

The raccoon looked up at Nate and hissed. Its forepaws, uncannily like human hands, twitched and flexed.

"I'll get him yet, for both of us," Nate said softly. The coon's small, dark, appealing eyes reminded him of something but he couldn't quite pin down the memory.

Shortly the animal broke into violent convulsions. Gasping loudly, the raccoon breathed its last and went limp.

Nate finished tapping the ball and wad down on top of the powder and slid the ramrod into its housing. He trailed the mountain lion a few dozen yards, seeking spoor, and wasn't overly disgruntled when he didn't find any.

The panther was as devious as it was bloodthirsty. Satan never made mistakes, never left enough sign for anyone to follow. Experience or an inherent disposition had transformed the mountain lion into a living engine of destruction with an instinct for self-preservation that bordered on the supernatural.

A wry grin curled Nate's mouth. He'd done it again, ascribed human traits to an animal. He must keep reminding himself that the panther was just that and nothing more. It could be killed just like any other panther. All he'd need was a bit of luck.

No. That wasn't quite right.

All he'd need was a *lot* of luck.

Chapter Seven

A deathly hush gripped the verdant woodland as Nate King hastened southward. It had been over an hour since he found the raccoon and not once had he so much as glimpsed the panther, but he knew the cat was close by, knew it was stalking him. Intuition, instinct, logical deduction, all were in harmony on that one point. Satan intended to slay him, and it was only a matter of time before the mountain lion tried.

Nate's senses strained to their limits. Often he paused to listen. His eyes constantly roved over the terrain, noting possible spots where the panther might jump him, spots to be avoided unless there was no choice, and in that case they were to be approached with the Hawken leveled and cocked.

Uneasiness rested heavily on Nate's broad shoulders. He was edgy and knew it. While not the sort to harbor irrational fears, he couldn't suppress a feeling that the worst was yet to come, that he might finally have met his match. Luck, more than skill, had seen him through numerous clashes with hostiles and beasts, and his luck in this instance seemed to have forsaken him. Already he'd lost all his horses and had to abandon his traps and other fixings. He was afoot, low on food. When he eventually became fatigued, he didn't dare lie down and sleep because he might not wake up again.

There was one bright note in the gloomy outlook. Nate would be safe once he reunited with Shakespeare McNair. He held that comforting thought uppermost in mind as he walked. It bolstered his confidence, allowed him to discount the early setbacks as minor occurrences. Then he came to the gorge.

As gorges went, this one was small. Narrow at the top, only two hundred feet from top to bottom, it nonetheless posed a formidable obstacle. Nate glanced right and left and was disheartened to see he would have to walk over half a mile in either direction to go around. Any delay at this point was costly since it meant he wouldn't rejoin McNair until well after dark.

There might be a means of gaining the far rim sooner. Nate turned westward, looking for a way down. He was beginning to regret taking the straightest course to save time. Just the opposite had happened. He would have been much better off going the easy way, as he had on horseback.

No means of reaching the bottom presented itself, but Nate was sure he spied a game trail in the midst of the heavy brush below, which meant there had to be a way. If so, it eluded him. He chafed with impatience and resigned himself to going all the way around.

Presently, Nate skirted an immense boulder balanced on the edge and stopped in delight on beholding recent deer prints leading over the rim. Sinking to one knee, he studied the side of the gorge. Long ago a section of wall had buckled, and now a steep slope consisting of crumpled rock and earth formed a treacherous incline dotted with many small boulders. The deer tracks wound to the bottom and disappeared in a thicket.

Nate started to ease over the edge, then hesitated. If he was wrong, if there was no way up the other side, he'd waste hours. Did he care to run the risk of another night alone? He glanced back, checked the forest for sign of the panther, and when assured it was safe to proceed, he carefully lowered himself onto the slope. Immediately a lot of dirt and small rocks cascaded out from under him. The footing was treacherous, maybe too treacherous, and he considered whether to climb back up and go on around just to be safe.

The sudden sound of onrushing feet alerted Nate to his peril heartbeats before Satan struck. Nate was in the act of spinning to confront the cat when his left foot slipped out from under him and he toppled backward.

The misstep saved Nate's life. He felt a puff of air fan his hair as the lion's paw just missed his head before the panther's body slammed into him. The impact bowled him over and he tumbled down the slope. Frantically, he tried to dig in his heels. He clutched at boulders but couldn't arrest his momentum. To the contrary, he fell faster, gaining speed the farther he went.

Nate involuntarily cried out when his left side smashed into a boulder. A bone distinctly cracked and the subsequent pain was enough to make his head whirl. The Hawken went flying. Nate hit another boulder, and another. Severely stunned, so disoriented he couldn't tell which way was up and which way was down, he continued tumbling end over end for an eternity.

A gut-wrenching impact ended Nate's descent. Dimly,

he was aware of loose earth and dust raining down upon him. Flat on his stomach, he tried to lift his head but couldn't. He was weak, his vision blurred. He also felt nauseous. Bile rose in his throat and he swallowed it. Gritting his teeth, he was about to try and sit up when he heard something coming down the slope toward him.

Satan!

Nate was in no shape to fight. He sucked in air and held it, then lay as limp as a wet rag, feigning death. His sole hope for salvation rested in convincing the mountain lion that he was dead. It might leave him alone if it wasn't hungry, although in light of its extremely bloodthirsty nature, that wasn't a certainty.

Light footfalls came close to Nate's head. Raspy breathing pinpointed the panther's exact position. Nate felt soft pressure on his shoulder and listened to loud sniffs. Warm breath touched his neck, his jaw, his cheek. The cat's face was inches from his own, so near its whiskers scraped his skin.

Stark panic welled up within Nate. It took every iota of self-control he had to keep from leaping up and striking out in blind terror. A paw nudged him once, twice, three times, and the third time claws bit into his flesh, not deep, but deep enough to cause him to bite his lower lip to choke off a yell.

Nate's lungs were at their limit. He had to take a breath, and once he did the mountain lion would be on him so fast he'd be unable to offer much resistance. The soft crunch of calloused pads worked their way toward his feet and he relaxed a smidgen, thinking Satan was going to leave. Suddenly tremendous anguish lanced his left ankle. Satan had bitten him! He almost screamed, but instead bit his lower lip and suppressed a shudder. Warm blood trickled down over his foot.

Satan gave another loud sniff, swatted the bloody moccasin once, and loped off.

Relief flooded Nate's being. His lungs were close to bursting but he held his breath a bit longer, afraid the panther would hear. Only when he was on the verge of blacking out did he swiftly cup a hand over his mouth to muffle the noise, then exhaled. His body shook as he gratefully gulped in fresh air while cautiously raising his head for a look around.

The mountain lion was gone, but whether up to the top of the gorge or somewhere in the brush along the bottom, Nate had no idea.

Nate saw an isolated pile of earth and stones nearby and dragged himself into its shadow. Propping his back against it, he took stock. His head hurt again, abominably, but there were no new wounds. His chest hurt, too, possibly from a fractured or broken rib. And there was his foot, which bothered him the least but was bleeding quite badly. Miraculously, neither the pistols, the butcher knife, nor his tomahawk had fallen loose during his headlong plummet, and the powder horn, ammo pouch, and parfleche were intact. The only item he'd lost was the rifle, the one he needed the most.

Nate peeled off his left moccasin and examined the puncture marks. The cat had nipped his flesh, no more, so the damage wasn't severe. Drawing his knife, he cut a wide strip off the bottom of his left legging and wrapped it tightly around his ankle. Several whangs tied into a long string sufficed to secure the bandage in place. He gingerly pulled the moccasin back on, drew a flintlock, and slowly rose.

There was still no sign of Satan so Nate shuffled to the slope and began climbing. He wasn't about to leave without the Hawken.

A rifle was an essential part of a trapper's gear, the single most indispensable item he owned. It enabled him to hold his own against fierce beasts and bloodthirsty hostiles. It made possible slaying game at distances no pistol could ever reach. Overall, a rifle made staying alive easier, and frequently was the deciding factor in whether a trapper lived or died.

Nate King intended to live. The only problem was that boulders covered the slope like warts on a toad, scores of them, and the incline itself was uneven, dotted with ruts and bigger depressions. The Hawken could be anywhere. He might miss seeing it even if he was right on top of it.

Climbing slowly, Nate peeked behind every boulder, in every crack. Thanks to the immense boulder at the top, the one he had been near when the panther attacked, he had a fair idea of the path he had taken to the bottom. Allowing for a five yard margin one way or the other, he could reasonably confine his search to a belt a dozen yards wide.

The climb became increasingly difficult the higher Nate ascended. He had to grab hold of boulders to keep his footing, and often he slipped despite the extra purchase. The loose earth slid out from under him no matter how lightly he set his feet down.

Sixty feet from the bottom the inevitable took place. Nate was easing around a boulder for a better look into a wide hole when the dirt underfoot swept out from under him and he fell backward. Arms flailing, he attempted to regain his balance. Gravity thwarted him, and he grimaced as he slammed onto his back and shot toward the bottom. Nothing he did stopped his slide. By twisting and turning he was able to avoid most of the boulders below him, but not all. At length he rolled to a stop in a choking cloud of dust, battered but not gravely injured.

Coughing and wheezing, Nate pushed to his feet and glared at the incline. It would be the height of folly to try again. Yet he refused to leave without the Hawken. If he could regain the rim, he might be able to spot it. But the only way to do that was to find a way up the other side and then to circle around.

Nate moved eastward, into the brush bordering the base of the south wall. The deer tracks led in the same direction. Too bad, he mused, that he didn't have tapered hoofs like they did; then he'd be able to scale the slope with ease.

A glimmer of blue was visible ahead. Nate ducked under a limb, passed a thornbush, and emerged in a clearing dominated by a picturesque spring. He squatted, tested the water by dipping a finger in and touching it to his lips, then drank his full. The spring explained why the deer visited the gorge regularly. They could eat, drink, and lie low, safe from predators.

Not now, though. Nate twisted and scanned the vegetation. Was Satan out there, watching him? Or had the panther gone elsewhere in the belief he was dead?

Pistol in hand, Nate entered the growth beyond the pool. The tracks brought him to a thin strip of bare earth adjoining the base of the wall. He was encouraged by the fact most of the tracks led in the same direction, which implied another way out of the gorge. In his eagerness to find it, he exerted himself more than he should have, and abruptly he was racked by intense spasms in his chest. Groaning, he doubled over, staggered to a low protruding finger of rock, and sat down.

The rib must be worse than he thought, Nate realized. It had been aching terribly since his second fall, but this was the worst yet. If he had any common sense he'd rest for a while to let the discomfort subside. But he was running short of time. Night loomed several hours off.

Nate picked up a thick twig, jammed it between his clenched teeth, and strode on. Whenever his ribs flared, he bit down hard. In this way he covered hundreds of yards and came to the path leading up to the south rim.

Actually, it wasn't so much a path as a series of skeletal switchbacks extending from the bottom to the very top, switchbacks wide enough for deer with their slender hoofs but hardly wide enough for a grown man's feet. Nate looked and would have swore if not for the twig in his mouth. The prospect of scaling them in his condition was daunting, but it was either that or attempt to climb the steep slope again.

Nate squinted at the sun, well on its western arc, then moved up the first grade to the sharp bend. Here the path was no more than six inches wide. He had to step sideways to get to the next grade. Treading with consummate care, he climbed to the second bend. Once more he moved sideways. And so on and so on it went until he was halfway to the top and half out of breath with his chest in acute torment. Halting, Nate leaned against the wall and stared at the switchbacks below. It was strange, but from that high up they reminded him of a series of steps, cellar steps, specifically, steps he hadn't thought of in many a year.

Long ago. Many miles away.

The boy sat at the bottom of the cellar steps, the club in his left hand, his bored expression fixed on a mouse hole in the wall beside his father's workbench. He heard footsteps above him but didn't turn around.

"Well, look at this, Sherm. He's still at it."

"The mice must be smarter than he is, Lou. That's all I can figure."

There were scornful snickers and a hand fell on the boy's shoulder.

"What the dickens is the matter with you, little guy?" Lou asked. "Over a week you've been at this and you haven't killed one lousy mouse."

"Keep it up and you'll spend the rest of your life down here," Sherm declared. "Father is so mad at you we can't even mention your name when he's around."

Hiding the ache in his heart, the boy shifted and gazed at his two brothers. "I haven't seen one yet."

"Don't lie to us, brat," Sherm said, giving the boy a slap on the back of the head. "We were all at the dinner table when father told us about the one you could have smashed but didn't." Smirking, Sherm leaned down. "Why didn't you? Were you afraid it would tear you apart?"

"Go away, Sherm."

"Don't tell me what to do."

Lou gave Sherm a shove. "Quit picking on him. Can he help it if he doesn't like killing things?"

"Yes, he can," Sherm snapped. "Think of how the other kids will act if word of this gets around. We'll never hear the end of their teasing."

"I'm the one they would tease," the boy noted.

"Wrong, milksop. We'd be picked on too because we're your brothers. Everyone will say it runs in the family, that the King boys must be girls." Sherm slapped the boy again. "And all thanks to you, you jackass."

"Father doesn't like us to swear," the boy said.

"Father isn't home right now," Sherm countered. He gestured angrily at the mouse hole. "What are you waiting for? Crush one of the damn things and he'll let you off the hook."

"I can't kill one if I don't see one."

Sherm bristled and would have jumped on the boy if not for Lou, who intervened by grabbing Sherm's wrists and holding fast. "I won't let you beat him up again. He's doing the best he can."

"Damn you both to hell!" Sherm said, yanking loose and moving to the next higher step. "You're always taking his side, Lou, even when you know he's wrong. He'd be better off if he didn't have you around to protect him. Maybe then he'd learn about life."

"Listen to you," Lou said. "Those are Father's words, not yours."

"They're true. He spends all his time with his nose buried in books. What's he going to amount to when he grows up?"

The boy stood and faced his brothers. "I don't know what I'm going to do," he told Sherm. "Sometimes I think I'd like to be a writer. Other times I think I'd like to work with figures since I'm good at arithmetic. And there are times, when I'm off hunting with Uncle Zeke, that I think I might like to live in the woods like an old hermit and have just the animals for company."

"You're touched in the head, you know that?" Sherm responded. "Zeke is a lot of fun, but he's missing a few marbles somewhere. And Father and him don't get along so well."

"I like him," the boy insisted.

Sherm started up the steps. "Do as you want, idiot. I've had my say." Stopping, he glared down. "But I'm warning you, Nate. If we get teased over this mouse business, I'm going to lick you proper."

"You can try," Nate said.

The door slammed behind Sherm. Lou sat down and crossed his arms over his knees. "Why make it worse by talking back to him the way you do? You know how he gets?"

"I should let him bully me all the time?"

"No. No, I guess not." Lou focused on the cause of the argument. "The whole family's upset, and all because of some stupid mice. Makes you wonder."

"I really will kill one," Nate mentioned.

"When?"

"When I have the chance."

Lou made a clucking sound. "Little brother, I come down here quite a lot to be alone, to think. I couldn't begin to count the mice I've seen when it's all quiet, especially at night. So tell me. And be honest. How many have you seen, just today?"

"Four."

"And you didn't club one?"

"I couldn't bring myself to do it." Nate held the club out as if about to cast it from him. "I know how easy it would be to bash in their skulls. I know they're just mice, and we can't have then overrunning the house. But they're living things, just like us."

"Wrong, little brother," Lou interrupted. "They're animals. We're not. They don't think like we do, don't feel like we do. They don't have souls like we do. You start making them equal with us and you might as well go live like a hermit because you won't be any better than they are."

"Are we better? Really and truly?"

"Dumb question. You like poetry. Know any mice that have written poems? Or painted beautiful art? Or sculpted statues?"

"But does that make us better?"

Lou cocked his head and regarded Nate quizzically. "Maybe Sherm and Father are right. Maybe you do read too much. How else would you come up with some of these crazy notions of yours?" Rising, he climbed to the door and paused with his hand on the latch. "You'd better get your thoughts straightened out. You say you like Uncle Zeke. Then remember what he told us about puny thinkers, as he calls them. There's a right way to think and a wrong way to think, and it seems to me you're in the wrong. Why, if everyone felt the way you do, we'd all be eating nothing but vegetables and fruit and we'd never have milk to drink or be able to go horseback riding. Gophers would ruin all the yards, cats and dogs would be living wild in the streets, and there'd be so many mice they'd be in your bath water." He opened the door. "You're smart enough to see the truth. You're just afraid to admit it."

Nate watched the door close quietly. As usual, Lou saw right through him and had hit on the heart of the problem. He took a seat on the bottom step, placed the club across his legs, and rested his chin in his hands. One mouse. All he had to kill was one mouse.

He stared at the hole and waited.

The switchback became harder to negotiate the higher Nate King climbed. Sometimes he had to leap over gaps, and at other times he had to cling to the gorge wall with his fingernails to keep from falling over the edge. His chest hurt worse as time went on, much worse, the pain so excruciating that he halted every few minutes to rest.

At long last the rim reared just twenty feet above Nate's head. Arm pressed tight against his ribs, he was making good headway when he came to where a four foot ridge of earth had buckled. There was no way to go around. He had to jump, so he moved to the very edge, crouched, and tensed his legs.

Movement in the gorge below drew Nate's attention to the spring. Barely controlled rage boiled within him as he watched Satan approach the pool and drink. There was the cause of all his troubles, and if only he had the Hawken he could have picked the panther off. He saw the cat sit and yawn, saw it idly gaze around and then look up. Right at him. Their eyes locked, and although the distance was too great for Nate to clearly see the mountain lion's features, he swore Satan's features lit with bestial glee.

Then Satan headed for the switchbacks.

Rather than be worried, Nate laughed. "That's it!" he declared. "Come on up here! By the time you reach the top, I'll be waiting for you with both pistols cocked. Come on!"

Thinking of how joyous it would be to plant two balls in the cat's brain, Nate leaped across the gap. Or tried to. Distracted by grand thoughts of rubbing his nemesis out, he failed to concentrate as he should have, and as a result he came down inches short of the other side. Mere inches, but it might as well have been miles. Quickly he thrust out both arms and caught at the lip. For a few seconds he held on, his legs flailing as he desperately tried to find purchase for them. His right moccasin found tenuous footing, and he was in the act of bracing for an upward lunge when burning agony seared his chest and made his head spin. Of a sudden he went weak.

Nate felt his fingers slipping and tried to gouge them into the soil. He kicked wildly but was unable to find solid footing. Panic tore at the core of his being. "No!" he cried, and helplessly plummeted over the side.

Chapter Eight

Blood rained out of a stormy sky, big, moist drops that splattered onto Nate King's face and beard and plastered his hair to his head. Blindly he struck at the dark downpour, striving to block the drops. Some got into his nose, some into his mouth. He sputtered, swallowed, gagged. High above him the storm clouds shifted, changing shape, transforming from simple clouds into a gigantic feline that snarled and hissed and clawed at him while a torrent of spittle, red spittle, showered from its mouth. "No!" Nate shouted, swallowing more damp liquid. "Stop it! Stop it!"

Suddenly Nate realized that he was sitting up and swinging wildly at thin air. Thunder rumbled overhead and raindrops were hitting his face. He blinked in confusion at the darkness enveloping him and wondered where he was until he remembered Satan and the pain in his chest and falling, falling, falling.

Nate groped the ground, looked down, then up. The

outline of the rim was faintly visible. He discovered he was still high on the gorge wall, on a switchback about fifty feet from the top. Had it not broken his fall, he would have been smashed to a pulp when he hit bottom.

Nate peered at the inky floor of the gorge and the lower switchbacks, puzzled by Satan's absence. The panther had been coming after him when he slipped. Why hadn't it finished him off? More importantly, where was it now?

A vivid bolt of lightning briefly lit up the heavens, attended by a tremendous clap of thunder. Nate was buffeted by winds so strong he had to hold on tight to keep from being plucked from his perch. The storm was intensifying. He had to reach the rim before the lightning or the wind accomplished what the fall had failed to do.

Rising to his knees, Nate winced as his chest again throbbed with torment. He tried to stand, but the instant he put his full weight on his left foot the leg was jarred by pain and he nearly buckled. Sitting once more, he gingerly felt his ankle and foot. Both were hugely swollen, whether as a result of the fall or due to the bite he had no idea.

Another jagged spear of lightning reminded Nate of his precarious position. Being so high up, he was a prime target. He had to find shelter swiftly.

Since he couldn't stand, Nate crawled up the grade, negotiated the switchback, and went on. His gravest worry was blundering onto one of the gaps and falling again. To prevent that from happening, he tested the ground ahead before advancing. This held him to a snail's pace but he would rather be safe than pay the ultimate price for being rash.

Gradually, painstakingly, Nate worked his way ever higher. The rain fell in buckets, drenching him to the skin. The lightning flashed continuously, the thunder boomed. Worst of all, the wind tore at him, trying to rip him loose and fling him to earth. His lips grim with determination, Nate kept on going.

The first gap Nate encountered was a small one, one he recalled from earlier, and was handily crossed. The next, being wider, took some doing. Nate had to inch both knees to the edge, guess where the upper incline was situated, and lunge at the same time he did a frog hop, throwing both arms straight out. He landed on firm ground and gave silent thanks.

At length Nate came to the gap where his mishap had occurred. He knew it was the one even though he couldn't see it clearly. Edging to the brink, he waited for another streak of lightning to illuminate the wall. In the garish glare, the gap seemed more like a chasm, an insurmountable gulf only a madman would try to hurdle. But hurdle it he must.

This time Nate focused on the patch of earth he must alight on and nothing else. Bunching his legs, he took a few deep breaths to compose his nerves, and when the next streak of lightning brightened the sky, he pushed off on his good leg, throwing himself across the open space as if shot from a cannon. Rain battered him, the wind lashed him, and then he was smacking down on his hands and knees and clinging fast to the slick, dank soil. He squatted there a while so his pulse would stop racing, then he crawled upward.

Many minutes elapsed. At last Nate attained the summit. He collapsed, exhausted, and shivered as the cold rain chilled him to the bone. Rousing himself, he limped into nearby undergrowth, into the densest bushes he could find, and curled up underneath them. Here the rain hardly touched him, the wind left him alone. He could relax for the first time since being attacked. Closing his eyes, he folded his arms across his chest and tried to rub warmth into his body. His rib was on fire, his left foot pulsing. Surprisingly, neither stopped him from promptly falling asleep.

Singing birds brought Nate around. He sat up, amazed to see the sky was clear, the day hours old. His chest didn't bother him as much but his foot was worse. One look was enough to show him why. Grinding his teeth so he wouldn't cry out, he pried his moccasin off and examined the discolored flesh. There was no doubt. The foot was infected.

Nate bowed his head, mentally resisting the tide of despair threatening to engulf him. A fractured rib, an infected foot, no rifle, low on food, and in dire need of water. What else could go wrong? Even though he had slept a long time, he felt extremely tired, and he wearily pressed a palm to his forehead. His brow burned with fever, hotter than it had ever been.

"Now I know," Nate muttered. He squeezed his foot into the moccasin, rose, and hobbled from the brush. Forest stretched southward into the distance. A short search turned up a broken limb the proper length, and using this as a crutch, Nate went on.

Reaching Shakespeare was more critical than ever. The mountain man had lived among Indians so long and learned so much from medicine men he knew more about healing than most doctors. Shakespeare would know how to treat the infection and tend the rib. All would be well.

Nate reassured himself with that thought repeatedly. But his condition steadily deteriorated. Presently he broke out in a sweat. His body would be hot one minute, cold the next. At times he wanted to throw off his buckskins, at others his teeth chattered.

A peculiar feeling seized hold of Nate, a lethargy so overwhelming he seemed to be moving in slow motion. It took forever for him to take a single step. His arms were so sluggish they were leaden.

Nate was familiar with the symptoms of tainted blood. He'd known a trapper who had succumbed after getting a foot caught in a trap. And there had been a Shoshone warrior, wounded by a Cheyenne arrow, who had died from the ailment. Certain herbs were supposed to be an effective treatment but he didn't know which ones they were.

Nate's sense of time was all askew. He plodded on because he refused to quit, relying on the crutch more and more. His leg was now swollen midway to the knee. In addition, his rib acted up again. And the whole time the fever raged.

Habit caused Nate to stop at noon and sit on a log. He closed his eyes, then jerked them wide when he began to drift off. He couldn't sleep yet. There would be plenty of time for that luxury once he found Shakespeare, which, if his strength held out, should be before nightfall.

While not hungry, Nate forced himself to eat to maintain his energy. The jerky tasted tangier than usual, making his mouth water. He stuffed a piece in his cheek, shoved up off the log. The top of his crutch had rubbed the skin under his arm practically raw, but it couldn't be helped. It was either go on or die.

Nate traveled southward for the longest time. His existence became a mechanical routine of forcing his good leg to take a step, then employing the crutch. Nothing else mattered. He had to reach Shakespeare and the only way to accomplish that was to keep on going even if his brow was hotter than a burning ember. His chest felt as if something was boring through his flesh from the inside out, and his left leg was in such pain he couldn't bear to put his foot down.

On and on and on Nate went. He was terribly thirsty but couldn't remember exactly where the streams were located. His mind was sluggish, almost numb. Conscious thought took so much effort he didn't bother thinking. He just plodded along, minute after minute, hour after hour.

At length Nate looked up and saw he was in a field of high grass. Bordering it to the south was a ribbon of a creek. The sight of cool, refreshing water sent a shiver down his spine. He cried out, a formless cry of hope and relief. From an internal reservoir he tapped the last of his waning strength and hurried forward.

A yard from the creek Nate let go of the crutch and threw himself flat on the ground. His lips touched the water and he drank as might a person who had been lost in a desert for a week. His thirst was unquenchable. He gulped and gulped until his belly bulged and he couldn't swallow another drop. Then he rolled onto his side and splashed water onto his fiery forehead and face.

It felt so indescribably wonderful to simply lie there and rest. Nate sank both arms into the creek up to the elbows, luxuriating in the chill sensation. He wanted to drink more but was afraid he'd be sick. Absently gazing skyward to learn how many hours of daylight were left, he was confounded to see the sun wasn't where it should be.

Nate had been heading south for ages. Or so he'd believed. The sun, therefore, should be to his right, to the west. Instead, the blazing orb hung in the heavens to his left. If the direction he thought was west was actually east, that meant he had either been walking in circles or had become completely switched around and been hiking northward for most of the afternoon.

"It can't be!" Nate declared as the full magnitude of his mistake hit home. He'd counted on finding McNair before nightfall. Now he didn't have the slightest idea which way to go. Was he still due north of Shakespeare's valley, or was he to the west or east of it? There were no landmarks nearby he recognized, no way to get his bearings.

I'm as good as dead! Nate reflected, and had to bite his lower lip as a flood of despondency rose within him. He closed his eyes and shook his head, fighting the feeling of hopelessness. He couldn't give up! He didn't want to die, not this way, not there, where no one would ever find him, not all alone, left there to rot and have his bones be bleached by the sun like that warrior whose remains he had found in the meadow. He'd never hold his beloved wife in his arms again or see his son and daughter. He couldn't, he wouldn't, let his end be so meaningless.

Nate sat up. He wasn't going to give up the ghost meekly. Since he could no longer count on being treated by his mentor, he had to quit being sorry for himself and treat his wounds the best he knew how. Shifting, he rested both feet by the creek. He tried pulling the moccasin off his left foot but the foot was now so horribly swollen he couldn't get the top of the moccasin down over his ankle.

The blade of the butcher knife gleamed in the sunlight when Nate pulled it from its beaded sheath. He removed the parfleche and stuck the strap between his teeth, then carefully worked the tip of the knife under the top of the moccasin. In order to cut the moccasin off, he had to twist the knife so the sharp edge was against the leather. Doing so produced waves of torment. Nate bit down on the strap, resisted the agony, and sliced away.

Winona had made the moccasins. The love she bore him, and the pride she had taken in her craftsmanship, were reflected in her work. The soles were exceptionally thick, the tops barely less so and quite supple. The moccasins had been made to hold up under the toughest of wear in the roughest of weather. Cutting through the leather was a chore for one as weak as Nate had become, but he persisted.

Perspiration dotted Nate's brow and made his buckskin shirt cling to his damp torso. He stopped cutting every so often to splash more water on his face. The moccasin loosened somewhat the lower he went, and after fifteen minutes was loose enough for him to remove, but only with great difficulty.

Nate's foot was ghastly. Discolored, two times its normal size, with a festering sore as large as his fist, it made his stomach churn to look at it. He lowered the foot into the creek and mustered a grin at the temporary soothing the water produced. Lying back, he closed his eyes. Before he knew it, he dozed off.

The caw of a raven woke Nate up. He sat, saw with a shock that twilight had descended. His foot had stopped hurting so he lifted it from the creek and examined the sore, which appeared to contain a pint of pus. He glanced at the knife lying beside him, then at the sore. His hand closed on the knife hilt.

Nate placed the parfleche strap in his mouth again, poised the blade over the sore. He hesitated, dreading what he had to do. Then, biting down hard, he jabbed the knife in. Two things happened simultaneously; the sore exploded in a sickening spray of yellowish-green pus and pain exploded in his head. He sagged onto his back, vainly trying to keep his wits about him. A dark veil enfolded his mind.

When next Nate opened his eyes it was night. The moon had risen and stars dominated the firmament. Wind from the northwest shook the trees and grass and fanned his hair as he bent forward to inspect his foot. The sore had drained of pus and was now deflated, thin shreds of skin hanging down. Some of the swelling had lessened and the pangs weren't as intense as they had been when he moved.

Nate soaked the slit moccasin in the water, then pulled it back on. He cut off more whangs and looped them around the top of the moccasin to hold it in place. Tucking the crutch under his arm, he stood. Since blundering through the woods in the dark tempted fate, he looked for a spot to curl up until morning. A small pine, its lower limbs eighteen inches above the ground, offered a haven. He crawled under, set both pistols in front of him so they were in easy reach, and rested a cheek on a forearm.

Nate's stomach rumbled with hunger but he made no move to open the parfleche. The little jerky and pemmican he had left might have to last him a long time. He would ration it and hope for a clear shot at game.

Having slept so much in the past twenty-four hours, Nate doubted he was tired enough to fall asleep very soon. He didn't take into account the ravaging effects of the rampant fever and the severe toll the hours of walking had taken on his weakened constitution. In no time at all he was snoring.

And dreaming. Adrift in a Stygian limbo, he felt something pulling at his leg, and when he looked down he beheld a tiny mouse nipping at his toes. The mouse grew in size, changing shape as it did. Suddenly the mouse was gone, replaced by a snarling monster, by Old Satan himself. Satan reared back on two legs to claw at Nate's face. Overcome by fright, Nate swatted at the panther's paws. His fingers were ripped off, leaving bloody stumps, and he was disemboweled. He opened his mouth to scream but no sound came out. Cringing in terror, he tried to flee and pitched into a black well. The mountain lion jumped down after him, coming closer, and closer.

The snap of a twig woke Nate up. Dawn wasn't far off. He saw a black-tailed doe at the creek, drinking. It was a perfect shot if he didn't scare it off. Moving slowly, he picked up a pistol and cocked the hammer. At the click the doe snapped its head on high, its ears swiveling, its nose twitching.

Nate fired but couldn't see if he'd hit the deer or not because the cloud of acrid gunsmoke hid it from sight. He blinked, coughed, snaked to one side, and was appalled to see the doe was gone. How could he have missed? The answer was that he couldn't, not at that short range, as he learned when he crawled out from under the tree and saw the twitching doe expiring in a growing crimson pool.

Forgetting the crutch, Nate limped over, drew his knife, and began carving before the doe stopped convulsing. He sliced off a patch of hide, lanced the blade deep into the flesh, and cut out a sizeable chunk. Ordinarily he would have taken the time to make a fire and to roast the meat until it was well done. Ordinarily, though, he wasn't this famished, this in need of nourishment.

Blood dripped from the chunk but Nate didn't care. He closed his eyes and bolted the meat cold, chomping as might a starving wolf. Gore and blood trickled down over his chin onto his throat and he wiped himself clean with the back of a sleeve. Seldom had a meal tasted so delicious.

Upon finishing that first piece, Nate carved out a second, bigger portion. Working as rapidly as he could, he got a fire going, transfixed the piece, and held it so close to the flames the outer surface was singed. His appetite had barely been whetted; he couldn't wait to dig into more. Mouth watering, he fidgeted and fussed over the meat until it was done. Then, unfazed by the hot fat that seared his palms, he gripped the portion in both hands and chomped down.

New vitality radiated outward from Nate's belly. Every morsel swallowed added that much more strength to his limbs. He felt like a new man when he was done, in spite of his chest and his leg. Moving to the creek, he leaned down to slake his thirst and had his good mood wrecked by a track imprinted in the mud to his left. It wasn't one of his tracks, nor one of the doe's.

It was Satan's distinctive paw print, so big no other panther in the Rockies could have made it.

Nate was jolted to realize the mountain lion had passed within a dozen yards of his hiding place sometime during the night. Thankfully the wind must have been blowing the other way or Satan would have detected his scent. He saw another track a few feet past the creek near where the cat had gone into the forest.

A new thought intruded itself. How far had Satan gone? Was the panther close enough to have heard the shot? Forgetting about a drink, Nate swiftly reloaded the spent pistol and crawled back under the pine. Maybe he could make the situation work in his favor. By lying low, he might be able to get a shot at the mountain lion if it came to investigate.

The waiting was harrowing in itself. Nate turned at every slight sound, jumped at the rustling of underbrush. The breeze now wafted into the forest, carrying his scent and that of the doe. Either or both should bring Satan on the run.

The better part of an hour went by and there was no sign of the cat. Nate concluded it was safe to ease into the open and was on the verge of sliding out when a chattering squirrel deep in the woods abruptly fell silent.

Nate flattened, went as rigid as a board, both cocked pistols in front of him. Satan was finally coming. He knew it in his marrow, knew he had to end their conflict while he was still invigorated from the meal and could still think clearly.

A fluid, tawny specter materialized in shadows fifteen yards away. Satan prowled in a half-circle, testing the wind, enticed by the intoxicating odor of fresh blood. Any other panther would have rushed into the open to tear at the doe, but not Satan. The panther had spent a lifetime cultivating caution and honing its feline instincts to an extraordinary degree. Satan's sensitive nostrils registered the hated man scent underlying the blood scent of the doe, and Satan knew that the two-legged creature he desired to kill was nearby.

Nate watched the cat pacing back and forth and had to curtail an impulse to fire. Satan needed to be closer for the pistols to be effective. He toyed with the notion of attempting to sneak up on the cat and wisely didn't. Let Satan come to him.

The panther paused, its blazing eyes raking the trees, the creek, the field. It snarled, not so much out of anger as to see what would happen. Oftentimes its snarl caused prey to bolt from cover, but not this time. The two-legged creatures never did as other animals would do. They were different, a challenge to hunt, to kill. Which appealed to his predatory nature.

The panther unexpectedly vanished and Nate scowled. Satan never did as Nate expected, never did the predictable. He intently scrutinized the vegetation. Nothing. He scanned low tree limbs since sometimes cats took to the trees. Nothing. He studied every bush close to the creek. Nothing. Then, anger getting the better of him, he glanced to his left and cursed under his breath. Or would have, had he not seen Satan on his side of the creek, eight feet off in the thick grass, staring right at him!

Their eyes locked, held. Neither moved. Nate wasn't sure he could get off two shots before the panther reached him and it would take both balls to bring the cat down. He lightly fingered the triggers, waiting for Satan to make the first move. When it came, it was so fast Nate was almost taken unawares even though he was ready for it.

One instant Satan was crouched in the grass, the next instant Satan was ducking under the low limbs to get at Nate and Nate was squeezing the trigger on his right flintlock. The pistol boomed, the cat recoiled, then leaped in again, paws flashing, claws extended. Nate raised the other pistol to put a ball in the lion's brain but the lion's paw was quicker. The pistol sailed out of Nate's grasp.

Scrambling backward, Nate threw the spent flintlock at Satan's head. He grasped his tomahawk, yanking it out as he rolled out from under the tree and rose. In the excitement of fighting for his life he forgot about his left leg, and when he stood, his leg gave way, causing him to stagger to one side, toward the creek, just as Satan charged.

Mountain Cat

Nate drew back the tomahawk, stroked it forward. The edge bit into Satan's skull but the angle was all wrong and it didn't slice in deep enough to stop the mountain lion. Satan slammed into Nate and they both crashed down, landing in the water, Nate on his back with the cat on top.

Nate King looked up into the contorted mask of ferocity incarnate and knew his end had come.

Chapter Nine

Certain moments in every man's life are so remarkably vivid, so profoundly intense, they are never, ever forgotten. Some are tranquil moments, such as the first time he is intimate with a woman or the birth of his first child.

Some are perilous moments, such as a knife fight, or being shot at, or set upon by savage beasts. These are events that call forth a man's courage, that test his manhood as few others can. In those moments of extreme danger when his life hangs in the balance, he is more totally alive than at any other time. Every one of his senses is at peak performance. His whole mental concentration and personal focus are on the danger at hand, and nothing else. He thinks deeply, feels deeply, lives deeply. If he survives, he reflects on them often, marveling at his deliverance, at the courage he didn't know he had before he was put to the test.

Nate King looked up into the snarling features of the creature about to slay him and was overcome, not by

116

abject fear, but by a calming courage. The panther was too heavy for him to throw off, especially as weakened and in anguish as he was. His arm holding the tomahawk was pinned under the cat's paw and he couldn't lift it. Kicking at the lion would only enrage it further and result in his innards being ripped out by its rear legs.

Nate saw Satan's wicked teeth lowering toward his jugular. He looked the panther in the eye and girded himself to die as a man should die, bravely and without complaint. There would be no screaming, no pleading, no whining.

No one was there to witness Nate's death. He had nothing to prove except to himself. The ultimate trial loomed and he accepted it as inevitable.

But at that very instant, the instant the panther's teeth were about to close on Nate's soft flesh, Satan suddenly straightened and glanced around. A shriek of pure rage was torn from the cat's lips and its tail whipped wildly. Then, in a single bound, it cleared Nate and the creek and landed at the edge of the undergrowth, into which it vanished.

Nate was too flabbergasted to move. He didn't realize he wasn't breathing until his lungs ached and he had to gulp in air. Dimly, he heard drumming, as of many hoofs. He tried lifting his head for a look but he was too weak to do so. The hoofbeats grew louder and louder, and Nate managed to twist his neck in time to see the best friend he had in all the world vault from the white mare and race toward him.

"Dear Lord! No!" Shakespeare cried, dropping to his knees in the water to prop an arm under Nate's shoulders. "How bad is it, son?" he asked. "Where did that panther get you?"

Nate was speechless with amazement. He was going

to live after all! His time had not yet come! A happiness so acute it brought tears to his eyes gushed up within him and he placed a hand on his mentor's arm.

Shakespeare, misconstruing, inquired anxiously, "Where does it hurt the worst? I don't see any blood."

"I'll live," Nate croaked huskily.

"That critter didn't get its claws into you?" Shakespeare asked in surprise. "You don't know how glad that makes this old coon. When I spotted you tussling with that thing, I figured you were a goner." He glanced at Nate's head, at Nate's left leg. "Seems to me you're battered up some, though."

"You don't know the half of it," Nate assured him.

The mountain man cracked a grin. "Well, now that you've had your yearly bath, what say we get you dried off?" Grunting, he got his other arm under Nate and stood.

"I can walk," Nate protested.

"Hush. I need the exercise." Shakespeare carried Nate from the creek and deposited him near the doe. "How thoughtful," he quipped. "You knew I was coming and wanted to have a meal ready."

Nate propped himself on his elbows. "How?" he asked.

"How did I find you? You can thank him," Shakespeare answered, pointing.

Twisting, Nate was shocked to see his black stallion standing with McNair's pack animals.

"He showed up in my camp all sweaty, about ready to keel over," Shakespeare explained. "Must have galloped the whole way from your camp to mine. I saddled up pronto, threw my peltries and fixings on the pack horses, and went to find you. Been looking every since."

The emotion in the older man's voice brought a lump to

Nate's throat. He swallowed, coughed, and commented, "You timed it just right."

"Not on purpose," Shakespeare admitted. "I found your camp easy enough, and I have to admit it worried me some seeing that dead horse and all that blood everywhere. I yelled and yelled and fired my gun but you never showed so I decided to track you down." His expression turned grimly serious. "It wasn't so hard at first. Then I came to that gorge where you took a tumble, and rather than go down in it, I rode all the way around, hoping I'd find where you came out. Sure enough, I did, but your tracks showed there was something wrong. You were walking unsteadily, and in a circle, no less. And now and then I came on the painter's prints." Shakespeare glanced at those by the creek. "Never set eyes on tracks so big in all my life."

"Satan would have finished me if not for you," Nate said softly.

McNair's eyebrow arched. "Satan? You've named it after that old legend?"

"It's fitting," Nate said. His rib acted up again and he had to lie back down. "I'll tell you the whole story as soon as I feel up to it."

"What's the matter?"

Nate explained about his rib. Shakespeare retrieved an old blanket which he cut into wide strips and wrapped tightly around Nate's chest. Shakespeare also bandaged Nate's head and applied an herbal paste to the punctured sore.

"I can't leave you alone for two minutes," the mountain man complained as he carefully bound the foot. "How in tarnation did you ever wind up tangling with that cat?"

While Shakespeare roasted venison and boiled coffee, Nate related his ordeal, concluding with, "I'm lucky to be alive, but I suppose I should count my blessings. I still have some hides left, and the stallion." He stared into the fire. "I only wish I hadn't lost my Hawken."

"That reminds me," Shakespeare said. Hustling to the far side of one of his pack horses, he was busy for a few moments. He returned proudly bearing a familiar rifle.

"You found it?" Nate blurted, half rising in his excitement.

"That I did, son," Shakespeare said, handing the Hawken over. "Spotted it from the top of that gorge. Had a hell of a time climbing down, I don't mind saying. Without my rope I never could have gotten to it."

Nate fondly clasped the rifle in his lap and stroked it as he might his wife's hair. "Thought I'd never see you again!"

"We can get attached to those things, can't we?" McNair chuckled, squatting beside the bubbling pot. "Here. How about if we warm your insides a mite?"

The coffee was perfectly delicious. Nate savored the first cup, sipping the potent brew and rolling it on his tongue. In a short time the venison was done and he ate with cheerful relish. The meat he had eaten earlier had only whetted his appetite. He was famished, as he demonstrated by gorging on half a haunch. When his stomach was full to bursting, he wiped his greasy hands on his leggings and settled back wearing a smile of supreme contentment. "Life doesn't get much better than this," he mentioned.

Shakespeare nodded. "We'll let you rest up tonight. Tomorrow is soon enough to go after your plews." He bobbed his head at his pack horses. "From what you've told me, I figure we should be able to pack them all onto my animals."

"If we can't, I'll tie the rest on the stallion," Nate suggested without thinking.

"And then what?" Shakespeare snickered. "Walk all the way back to your cabin with your leg in the shape it's in? You'll have to have it amputated if you try a featherbrained stunt like that."

"I won't leave any of my hides behind," Nate insisted.

"Quit fretting. You won't have to. We can always rig a travois if there are too many."

Nate hadn't thought of that. Indians used travoises all the time to transport their lodges, personal possessions, even their small children. The contrivances were ingenuously simple. First a pair of long poles were tied crosswise behind a horse's head. Next, behind the animal's rump, a pair of crosspieces were lashed a couple of yards apart. A latticework of thin but sturdy branches and buffalo tendon was constructed, forming an ideal platform on which to carry anything under the sun. "Good idea," he said.

"I like to have one at least once a month. Keeps me on my toes."

Somewhere in the forest a twig snapped. At the sound Nate sat up as if hurled from the ground by the grass itself. He cocked and pointed his rifle at the trees. Eyes narrowed, he raked the woods, his finger nervously rubbing the trigger.

"A bit jittery, aren't you?" Shakespeare commented.

"It could be the panther."

"It could be a chipmunk."

Slowly Nate lowered the Hawken and with marked reluctance let down the hammer. "We can't be too cautious where Satan is concerned."

"This panther really has you spooked, doesn't it?"

"If you'd been through what I've been through, it

would have you spooked too."

"I suppose," Shakespeare said, pressing his tin cup to his lips. Over the rim he studied his young companion closely. "I knew a free trapper once who let himself get spooked by a glutton," he remarked as he put the cup down.

"Oh?" Nate responded absently. A glutton, as he well knew, was a common nickname for the wolverine.

"Yep. He had himself a nice little dugout in Flathead country and had done real well raising beaver that year. One day he came home and found that something had broken in and made a mess of his fixings. The tracks told him it had been a wolverine. He was mad enough to spit nails, but he didn't think much else of it at the time because it's not out of the ordinary for a curious critter to make itself at home in a lodge or cabin or whatever." Shakespeare paused. "Then one day he came home again and found the same thing had happened."

"What did he do?"

"What you or I would have done. He set traps around his dugout and baited them with fresh meat. Damned if the glutton didn't swipe the bait without being caught." Shakespeare poured more coffee for both of them. "That wolverine grew fond of the trapper's place and came around every chance it got. Scared off some of his horses, ate every scrap of food it could find, and had the annoying habit of biting holes in his buckskins and blankets."

"Didn't he get a shot at it?" Nate wondered, now interested in the outcome.

"He tried. Mercy, how he tried. He became outright obsessed with rubbing that glutton out. Stopped trapping entirely. Hardly ever hunted. All he could think about was that furry varmint and how to go about killing it."

"Did he, finally?"

"No one ever knew. Came a time when a bunch of us stopped at his dugout to see him and he wasn't home. From the evidence, we guessed he hadn't been there in ages." Shakespeare took a swallow. "But we found plenty of wolverine sign."

Nate supported himself on an elbow. "You never tell one of these yarns unless you're trying to get a point across. Are you saying that I'm acting the same way toward Satan as your friend did toward the glutton?"

"Let's just say my yarn, as you call it, could be taken as a warning."

"You wasted your breath. I'm not about to go crazy on you over an ornery panther."

"I hope not."

Nate laughed and forgot about the matter until later that night when Shakespeare was snoring on the other side of the fire and sleep eluded him. He gazed thoughtfully at the star-dotted canopy overhead. No matter how hard he tried, and he was trying, he couldn't put the mountain lion from his mind. Over and over again he relived that last attack, relived being knocked onto his back in the creek and staring up into the cat's bestial features as its fangs dropped to his neck.

Why couldn't he shake the memory? Nate mused. It wasn't as if he hadn't been attacked by wild animals before. Bears, wolves, snakes, name it and he had found himself on the receiving end of their wrath. So why did Satan bother him so? The idea of the panther going unpunished after all that had happened agitated him terribly.

It was foolish.

Wasn't it?

*   *   *

David Thompson

Many years before. New York City.

The boy named Nate was crouched on top of his father's work bench, the club clutched in his right hand. He stared at the mouse that had emerged from the hole moments ago and a tingle of excitement rippled through him. Here was his chance! All he had to do was jump and swing.

Nose twitching, the mouse warily approached the cheese. It took a nibble, then another, and began eating in earnest, convinced it was safe.

Nate balanced on his heels, tensed to leap. Then he mentally pictured the end result of his club crashing down on the rodent's head, and he hesitated. The creature was so small, so very innocent. How could he take its life? Why didn't his father just plug up the holes so no mice could enter the house? That would be better than pounding this one to a pulp.

A second mouse appeared, poking its head out and looking right and left. Seeing its fellow eating the cheese, it dashed out to join in the feast.

Nate remembered his father's words: "Where there's one mouse, there are always more. If we don't prevent it, they'll overrun the house in no time. Your mother will find them in the pantry, in the flour, in the bread. Mouse droppings will be everywhere." Here was living proof his father had been right, yet still Nate couldn't bring himself to jump.

What's wrong with me? Nate quizzed himself. Was he so weak-willed he couldn't do what had to be done? Was he a puny thinker, as his Uncle Zeke described some people who didn't see things the way they were? He thought of Percy Bysshe Shelley and his other poetry books and was staggered by a mature insight; poetry, grand, glorious poetry, those golden words he loved so much, had no bearing at all on the day to day things that people did. Poetry didn't put food on the table, or keep a person clothed, or teach someone how to deal with vermin.

As if to prove that point, one of the rodents below paused in its chewing long enough to excrete waste.

Nate's mouth curled in heartfelt disgust. For the first time in his young life he looked at another creature and felt an urge to kill. Legs uncoiling, he sprang, swinging as he dropped. It was ridiculously easy. The first mouse had no inkling of danger and died with cheese bulging its cheeks. The second mouse froze, petrified with terror, giving Nate an opportunity to dispatch it with a single blow. He stood looking down at them, then hefted his club and smiled.

It took only a minute to reach the front room where his father sat reading a newspaper. His father glaced at him, saw the mice dangling by their tails from his hand, and frowned. "You should have known better than to bring them up here. What if your mother saw them?"

"I knew she's off shopping. And I wanted you to see."

"You did the job you were supposed to do. What do you want? A pat on the back?"

"I killed two of them."

The father folded his paper and regarded the boy a moment. "What did you kill, son?"

"Sir?" Nate responded uncertainly.

"What did you kill?"

The answer was so obvious that Nate was at a loss to understand why the question was even asked. "Two mice, Father."

"Look at them."

Nate did as directed, noticing how the brains of one trickled from its split skull. To his surprise he didn't feel queasy.

"What do you see?"

Confused, Nate studied them intently. What was he supposed to see? "Two dead mice."

"Nothing else?"

"No. Just two dead animals."

"Then what was all the fuss about? Why did it take you so long to do a simple chore?"

"I told you, Father. I've never killed before."

"How do you feel now that you have?"

"I'm glad I did as you wanted."

"You don't regret killing them?"

"No. It had to be done, just as you said."

His father smiled, a rare genuinely warm smile, and beckoned Nate closer. He draped a hand on Nate's shoulder and gave a gentle squeeze. "Remember this lesson, son. There's an old saying that life isn't a bowl of cherries, and nothing could be truer. We have to work hard to get what we want in this world. We have to overcome difficulties every step of the way." He nodded at the mice. "Often there will be things we don't want to do, don't like doing at all, but they have to be done whether we like doing them or not. The measure of a man is that he accepts his responsibilities and performs them without complaint. Do you understand?"

"I think so."

"Excellent. Now take those mice out back in the alley and leave them there for the cats."

"Sir?"

"You've seen how many cats and dogs run loose in this city, haven't you?"

"Of course. There must be hundreds."

"Thousands," his father corrected him. "All because people won't take responsibility for their pets. They let them breed like rabbits, and when they have too many, they just throw those they don't want out on the street where the animals have to fend for themselves." He lowered his hand to his lap. "It was different when I was young. Back then if people had too many cats or dogs they just took them and drowned them in a bucket or bashed their brains in. We didn't have the problem New York City has now with strays."

"So you want me to leave these mice for the cats to eat?" Nate said, amazed by this rare display of kindness.

"I want you to stack those old crates we have out in the alley and hide behind them. When a cat comes to eat the mice, you club it to death. Kill as many cats as you can before the mice are all gone."

"Sir?"

"Are you hard of hearing?"

Nate stared at the mice, at his club. "Oh. I'm to use the mice as bait like I used the cheese."

"You're learning." His father picked up the newspaper and went to unfold it.

"Can I ask you something?"

"Yes."

"Why do you want the cats killed?"

"There always has to be a reason with you, doesn't there?" His father tapped the paper. "Very well. Of late some cats have taken to standing on the fence late at night and caterwauling so loudly the racket wakes your mother. Then she has a hard time falling asleep again. Perhaps if we kill a few of the cats that call the alley their home, the caterwauling will stop."

Nate remembered their first talk about the mice. "So you want me to do this for Mother's sake, just like you wanted me to kill the mice for her sake?"

"You find that odd?"

"I just figured I was doing it for you."

"Would that make a difference?"

"No, sir."

"I'm glad to hear it. As for your mother, one day you'll have a wife of your own and then you'll understand why everything I do is for her benefit."

Nate was stunned. Clearly his father bore his mother tremendous affection. He had never given much thought to how much his parents loved one another. Based on all the arguments they had, he'd assumed they barely tolerated each other.

"A husband owes it to his wife to provide things like a decent home and fine clothes," his father was saying. "And to do all the little things he can to make her life easier. Of course, don't go overboard."

"Sir?"

"Like everything in life, women have their proper place. Take this business about granting them the right to vote. Whoever heard of such nonsense? Their minds are too shallow to grasp the complexities of politics. Can you imagine your mother casting an intelligent vote for mayor or president?"

"Yes," Nate said.

His father stared at him, then sighed. "Just when I was beginning to think there was some hope for you." He made a shooing motion with his hand. "Off with you, son. Do as I told you. And don't bother bringing the dead cats in to show me. Just pile them in the back yard and I'll count them later. I don't know if I can trust you to give an accurate tally."

"Whatever you say, sir," Nate responded, turning away quickly so his father wouldn't see the feelings his face betrayed. The mice in one hand, the club in the other, he ran from the house as if the fires of Hell were lapping at his heels.

Chapter Ten

"Watch out below," Shakespeare McNair shouted, and clamped his hands on the rope to stop the bale's descent. He waited until Nate moved aside, then continued lowering the hides to the ground. Once they were down, Shakespeare let the rope slip over the top of the stout spruce limb that had supported the bale's weight. He watched it fall, grasped the limb, and cautiously descended.

"This is the last of them," Nate said.

"Thank goodness," Shakespeare said, running a palm across his perspiring forehead. "If you ask me, I think you got yourself hurt just so I'd have to do all the heavy work."

"How did you guess?" Nate responded with a smirk.

"What's left?"

"We already have my fixings, so that leaves the traps."

"Where'd you hide them? On top of some mountain, I suppose?"

"In a thicket nearby. I'll show you."

Shakespeare picked up the heavy bale and threw it over his left shoulder with an ease belying his advanced years. "We'll have to go slow on our way back. My pack horses are going to tire easily toting as much as we have."

"We could leave some of my belongings here," Nate proposed.

"Be sensible. If you leave your traps, you run the risk of them rusting out on you unless you cache them good and proper, which is more bother than it's worth where traps are concerned. You can't afford to lose your packs and parfleches so we have to take them. And we sure as blazes can't leave your hides."

Nate didn't disagree because he knew his friend was right. Still, he felt uncomfortable putting Shakespeare to so much trouble. He held the Hawken in both hands and hopefully surveyed the valley.

"Still looking for that painter?" Shakespeare commented, chortling. "You just can't let it rest."

"You wouldn't either if it had happened to you."

The mountain man squinted at the younger man. "Don't get your britches in an uproar. I didn't mean to imply you haven't been through the wringer. But we haven't seen hide nor hair of Satan since that tussle you had at the creek. He's long gone and not likely to bother us again."

"You're wrong."

"How so?"

Nate didn't take his eyes off the forest. "Satan is in this valley somewhere. It's his home, his sanctuary. He's out there right this second spying on us, just waiting for his chance to sneak in close and do us harm. I know he is. I can feel him in my bones."

"If you ask me, son, you're getting a bit carried away with this whole affair," Shakespeare cautioned. "You've been making this Satan of yours out to be some kind of demon, and he's not. He's no different than any other painter."

"You don't know him like I do. You haven't seen him up close. He's not a demon, but he is the biggest panther that ever lived, and the smartest, too."

"Crafty, maybe, but not smart in the same way people are smart. There's no denying that animals can be clever sometimes, especially those that have to prey on others to get a bite to eat. But you're still ten times smarter than this Satan."

Nate didn't reply. He knew his friend was wrong, but how did he go about convincing a man who had dwelled in the Rockies more years than Nate and his wife combined had lived that this mountain lion was unique, a rare specimen endowed with unmatched cunning and viciousness? Engrossed in his thoughts, Nate emerged from the last rank of spruce trees and saw all the horses gazing intently eastward. He did the same and drew up in midstride.

Satan stood by the stream less than a hundred yards off, head held low, tail swishing slowly. Evidently he had been working his way toward the clearing.

Dashing to the left for a better shot, Nate rammed the Hawken to his shoulder and tried to take a bead. Satan foiled him by bounding across the stream and into saplings lining the bank. "Damn!" Nate fumed. Spinning, he ran to the black stallion and vaulted into the saddle. A jerk of the reins and the stallion erupted in a gallop, speeding along the stream toward the spot where the panther had disappeared.

"Nate! Wait!" Shakespeare called.

The shout was wasted. Nate was only interested in one thing. Disregarding a lancing pain in his chest, he forded the stream and raced to the edge of the slender saplings to where he rose in the stirrups to try and spot the panther. Again he was foiled. It had only taken him twenty seconds or so to get there, but Satan was nowhere in evidence.

Nate circled the saplings, hoping against hope the cat was hiding in the stand. A complete circuit turned up nothing, not even tracks. Chagrined by Satan's escape, he rode slowly back to the clearing and dismounted.

"I could have told you that you were wasting your time," Shakespeare said, and received a glare that would have withered a plant.

"You could have helped. You could have gone to the other side of the stand to cut him off."

"Wouldn't have done any good," Shakespeare said, refusing to be ruffled. "I spotted the painter running off through that thicket north of the saplings as you were riding up to them."

"Why didn't you say something?"

Shakespeare shrugged. "I figured it wouldn't have done any good. As touchy as you've been acting today, you'd have ignored me."

"I have not become—" Nate began, and caught himself. He wouldn't insult McNair by lying to him. Especially not when his friend was telling the truth. He had indeed been irritable, ever since they entered the valley, and it didn't take a genius to figure out why.

"Let it go, son," Shakespeare said kindly.

"I don't know if I can," Nate said, limping toward the thicket. He'd forgotten all about his foot in the excitement and now he felt as if someone was repeatedly stabbing it with a dagger made of living fire. Grimacing, he checked the position of the sun, saw there were only two hours of daylight left. "We'd better hurry if you want to put this valley behind us by nightfall."

"Point to the traps and I'll fetch them."

"I'm not helpless," Nate grumbled. Ducking low, he worked his way to the Newhouses. Three trips were needed to bring them all out. As he assisted in tying them onto the pack animals, he looked at his mentor. "I've been thinking."

"A dangerous habit," Shakespeare said, and quoted his namesake. "Heaven make thee free of it."

"You haven't heard me out."

"I don't need to."

"Are you clairvoyant now? Do you know my thoughts before I speak them?"

"I know you, young sir."

"You think you do."

Shakespeare became somber. "Methinks I am a prophet new inspired, and thus expiring do foretell of him. His rash fierce blaze of riot cannot last, for violent fires soon burn out themselves."

"Are you talking about me or the damn panther?"

"Perhaps both. Perhaps neither."

Nate finished tying a sack and turned. "I hate it when you talk in riddles."

Soon they were ready to depart. Nate assumed the lead, a pack horse trailing his stallion. The Hawken rested across his thighs, handy for immediate use. He scoured the adjacent slopes, the woodland, the open spaces. Deep down he knew without a shadow of a doubt that Satan was observing their every move, and all he asked for was a single good shot.

They were in an unspoken race with the sun but they couldn't ride as fast as they would have liked, not with the pack horses so overburdened. And, too, Nate deliberately went a shade slower than he might otherwise have done in order to increase his chances of spying the mountain lion. As it was, despite this, they would have reached the crest of the ridge bordering the valley to the south if not for an unexpected occurrence.

Nate was seeking a shorter route to the ridge when he saw a large brown animal move in pines to the southwest, across the stream. Automatically he brought the Hawken to bear in case it was a grizzly. Seconds elapsed, and the animal stepped into the open and lowered its muzzle to graze on grass. "My other mare!" he blurted, drawing rein.

Shakespeare came alongside. "She's lucky the painter was busy dogging you or she'd be a goner by now."

"We need her," Nate declared, transferring his lead rope to McNair. He moved to a pack animal and removed another rope from a pack. "Take care of the rest. This shouldn't take long."

"You never know. She's been running wild for a few days. Sometimes being free gets into their blood."

"The stallion can catch anything," Nate boasted. However, in order not to wear the black out in a long chase, he bent low over the saddle and took advantage of all the cover available until he reached the stream. Here he had no choice. Galloping into the open, he crossed the stream in a spray of water and gained the opposite bank. It was then that the mare bolted, mane and tail flying as she fled eastward.

Nate applied his heels and pursued. He had to catch her for her own good. As Shakespeare had noted, now that Satan was roaming the valley again, it was only a matter of time before the panther found her.

The mare, however, evinced no desire to be caught. She stuck to flat, open country, to the high grass, leaving a path of flattened stems in her wake.

As usual, the black stallion responded superbly to the challenge. The horse loved to run, loved to put its strength and endurance to the test. Head low, muscles rippling, the black gradually narrowed the gap.

Nate was holding the Hawken in his left hand. He now transferred it to his right, the same hand holding the reins, to free his left for slipping the rope over the mare's neck. Ahead, the mare glanced back, saw they were gaining, and went a smidgen faster. Nate did likewise, constantly scanning the ground for animal burrows or other holes or ruts that might pose a danger to the stallion. He could ill afford to lose the black to a busted leg.

The mare displayed surprising stamina. A full mile had fallen behind them when she finally began to show fatigue and slowed slightly. This was the moment Nate had been waiting for, and he let the stallion have its head. The mare swerved as they swooped toward her, swerved again when Nate came near enough to swing the loop at her.

"Hold still!" Nate bellowed, leaning far to the side. He almost got the rope over her but she angled away, abruptly wheeled, and galloped westward.

"Contrary cuss," Nate muttered, hauling on the reins so the stallion would turn. Again he overtook her, again she cut to one side. He remembered the time his family had visited Santa Fe, remembered seeing *vaqueros* at work on a nearby ranch, and wished he knew how to use a rope, or *reata*, with the same skill they did. He'd have the mare caught in no time.

Although winded, the mare had enough spunk to keep

dodging and weaving. Nate reached the limits of his patience and stopped. So did the mare, twenty yards off, her head drooping as she breathed noisily.

Nate was about to try a ploy that might bring success. Most horses, when goaded into motion, started out briskly enough, then picked up speed as they went. Some, like the black stallion, had a knack for vaulting into a full gallop the instant they were urged to do so. He gave the stallion a few pats, adjusted the rope so the loop was by his leg, then jammed his heels in and hollered, "Heeeyaaah!"

The stallion streaked like an arrow at the mare. She snorted, tried to flee, but this time she was much too slow. Nate flashed next to her, his arm flicked out. The noose sailed over the mare's head, tightened on her neck, and Nate had her. He yipped like a Shoshoni, exuberant.

Once she was caught, the mare's resistance evaporated. She followed docilely as Nate headed back. He noticed deep slash marks on her hindquarters made by Satan that night in the clearing. They were healing nicely, and in a couple of weeks she would be as good as new.

By now the sun had dipped close to the horizon. Nate knew they would be unable to leave the valley before darkness set in but he wasn't upset. Rather, he looked forward to spending one more night in Satan's domain since there was every likelihood Satan would make an appearance.

As Nate rode, he pondered memories long neglected.

Years before. A cluttered alley in New York City.

The stacked crates formed a wall on three sides, while behind Nate was the fence. He had left a gap so he could dash out and brain any cats that strayed by, and for half an hour he had crouched in readiness, doing his best to avoid looking at the pair of dead mice.

His young mind had been whirring with new thoughts since his conversation with his father, thoughts he dared never voice in front of his father for fear of receiving a dreaded visit to the woodshed.

Minutes ago Nate had made a decision. To him, it was no different from the dozens of decisions he had to make each and every day, no different than deciding which clothes to wear or which book to read next. Had he been a little older, he might have realized this wasn't the case. No, this decision was exceptional, one of the most important any person could make. He didn't know it at the time, but it would have a profound impact on his life later on, when he was older, on the verge of manhood.

Presently Nate spied a pair of cats prancing down the alley toward him. He grasped the club, dipped lower, only an eyeball peeking out. One of the cats was yellow, the other brown. Both were lean, much leaner than house cats normally were.

It was the yellow cat that caught sight of the mice first. Pausing, it sniffed the air, looked all around, then ran to the rodents and took one into its mouth. Its companion dashed to the second mouse, bit down.

Neither feline saw Nate. Neither suspected he was there. Nate rose slowly, raised the club on high. He looked at the yellow cat, then the brown one. His shoulders bunched and he swung, driving the club down onto the crates, smashing so hard he cracked the wood.

The crash startled the cats, caused them to leap away, to fly for their lives with their prizes clutched in their jaws. Neither so much as glanced back.

Smiling, Nate stepped through the gap and stared at

smears of blood in the dirt where the mice had been lying. He went into the back yard, tossed the club down, and marched into the house, straight to the room where his father still sat reading the newspaper. His father looked up.

"You killed one already?"

"Not exactly, sir."

"Then why are you inside?"

"I made a mistake."

The paper was forgotten. "What kind of mistake?"

"I lost the bait."

"The mice? How, pray tell?"

"Some cats took them."

"You didn't use your club?"

"I swung," Nate said. "But you know how fast cats are. I'm sorry, sir. They got away."

His father's displeasure was transparent. "I suppose I shouldn't be surprised. I'm disappointed, though. I expected better of you."

"Do you want me to kill more mice and try again?"

"What would be the use? No, I'll have your brother Sherman attend to the cats. He knows how to follow instructions to the letter."

Nate had to secretly pinch his leg to keep from cracking a grin.

"Tell me the truth, son," his father said.

"Sir?" Nate responded, feeling a rush of fear. Did his father suspect?

"You weren't paying attention to the job you had to do, were you? You were daydreaming and let those cats sneak right up to the mice. Am I right?"

"No, Father. I would never do that."

"Be honest with me, son. I won't punish you for telling the truth."

"I saw them coming. Two of them. I swung the club just like I said."

"And missed." Somehow his father contrived to make the two words a harsh rebuke. "When will you learn, Nathaniel? How soon before you start acting your age? There's a right way and a wrong way to do everything in life, and you have to learn how to do things the way they should be done."

"I'm trying to do what is right. Believe me, Father. There's nothing I want more."

"I'm very pleased to hear you say so. Perhaps there's some hope for you yet."

"Thank you. I sure hope there is."

His father stood and stretched. "Well, what's done is done. Run along and find something useful to do. Don't bury yourself in those ridiculous poetry books your mother is so fond of."

"Never again."

"What?"

"I'm tired of them."

"Since when?"

"Since today. I think I'll read that book you've been wanting me to read, *Robinson Crusoe*."

"An excellent choice," his father declared, placing a firm hand on Nate's shoulder. "I'm quite delighted. To you this might seem insignificant, but you've taken a big step toward manhood today."

"By giving up poetry?"

"There's a fine line between being a boy and being a man. You cross that line when you're willing to relinquish the silly ideas and things of your childhood and devote yourself to mature pursuits."

"And when we learn the difference between right and wrong," Nate reminded him.

"That too, son. That too."

*   *   *

Nate King sipped his coffee and stared across the blazing fire at his mentor. Since sundown he had been wrestling with his decision and how best to convince McNair. He cleared his throat and began by remarking, "Do you think that it's hard sometimes for a person to tell right from wrong?"

"Here it comes," Shakespeare said, leaning back against his saddle.

"Here what comes?" Nate asked in feigned innocence.

"You've got it into your head that you have to rub out Satan and you're about to give me your reasons."

Nate was impressed. "You really are clairvoyant."

"Balderdash. You're as obvious as a pimple on a baby's bottom. But go ahead anyway, if it will make you feel better."

"You don't agree it has to be done?"

"I haven't heard your reasons yet."

"There's only one that counts," Nate said. "Satan is a man-eater. I'm sure of it. If we don't put him under, one day another trapper will wander into this valley and his death will be on our heads."

"Ahhh." Shakespeare stared into his cup and swirled the coffee. "Whether 'tis nobler in the mind to suffer the slings and arrows of outrageous fortune, or to take arms against a sea of troubles, and by opposing end them."

"I say we take arms."

"And our pack horses? What do they do while we're off chasing your fiend?"

"One of us will have to stay with them at all times."

"Which one?"

"I'm the one Satan nearly killed."

"Figured as much," Shakespeare said, and fluttered his lips in vexation. "I do beseech you, by all the battles wherein we have fought, by the blood we have shed together, by the vows we have made to endure friends, that you directly set me against this hellish cat."

"I'm the one," Nate insisted.

"But your foot? Your head? Your rib?"

"He's hurt too. I think I put a ball into him, and I know I landed a solid blow with the tomahawk. We'll be fairly matched."

"Fair?" The mountain man snorted. "A fool in good clothes, and something like thee. 'Tis a spirit: sometime it appears like a lord; sometime like a lawyer; sometime like a philosopher."

"I've lost your trail."

"A painter knows nothing of fairness. To Satan life is survival, and he'll do whatever it takes to survive. He knows the valley, you don't. His senses are ten times sharper than yours. He can move like a ghost, you can't."

"Is this your way of boosting my confidence?" Nate joked.

"It's my way of saying you're loco."

Nate set his cup on a flat rock and gave his friend a searching look. "When I was a kid I learned that a person has to do what he or she thinks is right no matter what the consequences might be. We can't live with ourselves otherwise." He paused. "We all have to answer for our actions in the end."

There was a long silence. Eventually Shakespeare McNair poked a stick into the flames and remarked, "We see it through, then, no matter what."

"No matter what."

Chapter Eleven

The Rocky Mountains teemed with life. Daytime or nighttime, various birds, mammals, and reptiles were always abroad. During the evening and morning hours the wild creatures were most noticeable since it was then that most ventured forth to forage for food and water.

One hour in every twenty-four was different, however. During that time the Rockies were unusually quiet, enjoying an atmosphere of well deserved serenity. It was the hour before dawn, when most of the nocturnal prowlers were retiring to their dens or burrows and the animals normally abroad during the day had not yet risen.

During this peaceful interval, the forest seemed to snatch a few precious moments of rest. Often the trees themselves stood straight and still, for even the wind died down during this time. Rarely did so much as a single bird chirp, or an insect buzz. Creation slumbered at the feet of its Creator.

Any noise, however slight, was like a gunshot in a library and instantly caught the attention of anyone or anything within earshot.

So it was that Nate King's eyes flicked open when his ears registered a sound his brain couldn't identify. He slowly sat up, prodding his sluggish mind to life, and gazed at the horses. When danger threatened, their keen hearing provided the first warning. But they were dozing, as they always were at this time of the morning. McNair dozed too, although he was supposed to be keeping watch.

Shaking his head at his edginess, Nate reclined on his side and tucked his hands under his chin. He hadn't slept all that well out of concern Satan would pay them a visit. That the panther hadn't shown puzzled him. Satan knew they were there, and Satan didn't tolerate intruders in the valley. The cat should have put in an appearance.

Nate considered waking McNair and teasing his friend about falling asleep, but didn't. Sunrise wasn't far off, as indicated by the pale shade of pink suffusing the eastern sky. Let Shakespeare get a few minutes of rest. They both needed to be at their best once the hunt began.

From upstream came a low sound, the same that had awakened Nate, and he lifted his head to listen. It was a swishing sort of noise, like the flurry of small wings. He mentally pictured a flock of sparrows taking wing, then realized the significance and rose to his feet, Hawken in hand.

None of the horses were agitated and Shakespeare slumbered on. Nate wondered if he was being unduly nervous again. He didn't want to raise a fuss and be made the fool when his fears proved groundless. Perhaps he should investigate first.

Nate padded to the stream and paralleled the bank.

David Thompson

The morning air was crisp and cold, chilling his lungs when he breathed. Dew clung to the grass, moistening his moccasins with every step he took. It was light enough for him to see several fish a few yards away, and to spot a lone bull elk in a clearing high on a neighboring mountain. He smiled, relishing the simple fact of being alive.

McNair's herbal remedies had worked marvels. Nate's leg was stiff, his foot a trifle sore. He still limped, but only a little. His rib ached dully, his head hardly hurt at all. Compared to his condition two days ago, he felt like a new man.

Nate covered a hundred yards without incident. The woods were as quiet as a tomb. Other than the bubbling of the stream, the world lay hushed, girded for the swirl of activity the dawn would bring. He halted, convinced he was wasting his time, and turned to go back.

The faint chittering of an early-rising chipmunk attracted Nate to a bald hillock to the northwest. He raked the hill, saw no reason for the chipmunk's agitation, and was twisting to continue walking when he beheld Satan and gasped. The panther was crouched on top of the hill, staring at him, its tawny coat blending into the background so well it was nearly invisible.

Nate brought up the rifle, then realized the range was too great for an accurate shot. "Stay there, you bastard," he said to himself. "I'm coming for you."

Shakespeare leaped erect when Nate flew into camp. The mountain man watched as Nate grabbed his saddle, and remarked, "Going somewhere?"

"I just saw the painter," Nate said, using the same word his friend and many of the old-timers did to refer to the big cats.

"You think you can catch it?"

"I'll try my best." Nate threw his epishimore on the stallion and smoothed it out. "With any luck I'll be back by noon, dragging that devil behind me."

"It might be wise to wait until there's more light."

"Satan will be gone by then."

"Maybe we could shoot a buck and hang it out as bait to lure him in close. Panthers love venison."

Pausing, Nate said, "We've been all through this. Quit worrying. I'm perfectly able to take care of myself."

"It seems to me that any man walking around with a busted rib, a bashed head, and a lot of teeth marks in his foot is playing fast and loose with the truth when he claims he's the careful sort."

"I have no time for this," Nate said. Every moment spent talking to McNair was another moment Satan had to get away. He placed the saddle on the epishimore and adjusted the cinch.

Shakespeare wore an unhappy expression. "I'd go with you if I could. You know that."

"I swear. Sometimes you're worse than a mother hen. Quit feeling guilty. One of us has to stay with the pack animals, as we decided." Nate mustered a smirk. "Just don't fall asleep again when you should be keeping watch."

"I still think I'm the one who should do the chasing. You're in no shape for a long, hard ride."

"We'll find out soon enough, won't we?" Lifting a foot to a stirrup, Nate swung up and gripped the reins. "Try not to get too bored. I'll return as soon as I can."

"Don't rush on my account," Shakespeare advised. "Shoot sharps the word."

"Don't I know it." Nate touched a finger to his brow, wheeled the stallion, and was set to gallop off when McNair said his name.

"Aren't you forgetting something?" Shakespeare held up a parfleche. "If you don't eat, you'll be too weak to hold your own against that varmint."

"Thanks," Nate said. He sheepishly took the bag and secured it to the saddle. They exchanged meaningful looks, then he was off like a shot, riding low over the stallion as the splendid mount sped along the south bank to the approximate spot where Nate had spied the panther. Much to his amazement, Satan hadn't moved.

The stallion took the stream on the fly. Nate couldn't understand why Satan didn't run off, why the big cat just sat there as Nate rode steadily nearer. He lashed the stallion with the reins, wishing it could go faster.

The ground leading up to the hillock was rocky, sprinkled with large boulders. Often Nate lost sight of Satan for a few seconds as he skirted them. A mere forty yards separated Nate from his quarry when, on going around yet another boulder, he saw Satan glide into pines on the north slope.

Nate angled to intercept the cat. He reached the base of the hill and plunged into the trees, alert for movement in front of him. When he saw it, it wasn't in front, it was to the right. Satan was in full flight, clearing twenty-foot stretches with prodigious leaps.

"Not this time!" Nate said somberly. He pursued, wending among the pines with reckless abandon, resolved to end Satan's life even if he had to chase the panther to the ends of the earth. The mountain lion glanced around, saw him, and ran faster, its fluid body a copper blur as it flowed over the rugged terrain with an ease few creatures could match.

The stallion knew what was required of it. On scores of occasions Nate had ridden down buffalo, elk and other game, and once the stallion knew which animal was being chased, it took to the challenge of the race with a passion almost human in its intensity.

Down the hillock. Across a grassy meadow. Up the slope of a mountain. Satan held to a straight course as if he had a definite destination in mind. Two hundred yards up the mountain, the cat bore to the east.

Soon Nate discovered why. The woodland gave way to a tract of land where a geologic upheaval ages ago had caused massive buckling. There were many steep gullies, treacherous washes, narrow ravines.

Nate suspected that Satan had chosen the area on purpose, knowing the stallion would be hard-pressed to keep up. Every gully, every wash, every ravine slowed the horse down, while Satan took each obstacle in stride, leaping from rim to rim where possible, skirting them with lightning speed where it wasn't.

No one would ever guess, judging from Satan's performance, that the cat had been shot at close range and struck with a tomahawk. Nate figured the shot had done no more than graze the beast, and the tomahawk must have only broken the skin.

For over fifteen minutes the mountain lion put a lie to the widespread belief among free trappers that panthers lacked stamina and would collapse after running short distances at top speed. Satan showed no sign of tiring and didn't stop until clear of the buckled landscape. Then he halted on a clear slope and looked back, tail switching like a whip.

Nate had lost considerable ground despite the stallion's valiant performance. He wanted to scream in baffled fury when Satan made for another expanse of forest. Once he lost sight of the panther, he might as well give up since tracking the lion to its den would be next to impossible. Either he caught up quickly or he would have to try again another time.

The stallion seemed to sense Nate's frustration and redoubled its efforts. Coming to the lip of a ravine, it vaulted high into the air, front legs tucked tight, completing an arc that brought it safely down on the opposite lip. Earth crumbled out from under its rear hoofs and for a couple of harrowing seconds Nate thought they would go over the side. But the black dug in its front hoofs, threw its weight forward, and galloped onward.

Presently Nate came to the forest and entered at the same spot as the panther. As he had dreaded, Satan was nowhere to be seen, nor were there any prints. The ground was too hard. He went a dozen yards, then worked in a half-circle, seeking tracks anyway, refusing to give up.

At length, thirty yards from the clearing, Nate came on a partial paw print in a patch of bare earth. It wasn't much, but it was enough to show Satan's direction of travel so Nate went the same way. Apparently the cat was heading higher, toward the lofty heights panthers invariably called home, perhaps toward its den.

Gradually the clustered pines gave way to scattered stands of firs interspersed with shimmering aspens. Above them grew dwarf pines, sprouting among a sea of boulders.

Nate drew rein at a boulder field and surveyed the steep slopes above. There had been no more prints to guide him. He was relying on intuition and logic. Somewhere up there Satan was holed up. He was sure of it. Locating the den was crucial.

A glint of white off to the right aroused Nate's curiosity. On riding over, he spied bones, reminding him of the dead Indian. The last thing he expected to find was more human remains, yet that was exactly what he had discovered. Dismounting, he knelt to examine them.

Another warrior had gone on to the realm of the Great Medicine Spirit. These bones were much older than the previous set. Nate estimated the Indian had died a year or so ago. The cause of death was easy to ascertain; there were teeth marks on the arm and leg bones and the skull had been partially crushed by immense iron jaws.

"Satan," Nate whispered to himself. He picked up the skull, turning it in his hands. What had the man been doing there? Hunting elk? Bighorn sheep? Or had he been after Satan and the panther had turned the tables on him?

Reverently, Nate set the skull down in the same exact spot and stepped back. "Rest in peace," he said softly. "I aim to rub out the hellion that did this to you."

Nate forked the saddle. Four or five hundred feet higher reared craggy cliffs, their seamed rocky surfaces glinting dully in the bright sunlight. He rode toward them, the Hawken resting on his thighs.

At this elevation the wind howled almost constantly, shrieking over the rim of the cliffs and sweeping down across the slopes below. Nate and the stallion were buffeted severely. In order to stop his eyes from watering, Nate tucked his chin to his chest and peered upward through slitted eyelids.

The cliffs formed a formidable wall extending over half a mile. Nate could readily imagine the number of secluded nooks, crevices, and caves there must be. Locating Satan seemed a hopeless chore, akin to finding the proverbial needle in a haystack. Yet he had it to do.

Nate tilted his head back to scour the stony ramparts as he drew nearer. Fifty feet from them he turned and bore westward, his eyes now glued to the dusty ground. A single track was all he needed to give him some idea of Satan's whereabouts, but he traveled a quarter of a mile and didn't see one.

The sun hung in the western sky when Nate came to where the cliffs tapered off. He slid down so the stallion could rest and sat with his back against a stunted tree, facing the ramparts. The whole day was nearly gone and he had failed to find Satan. He might as well return to camp and resume hunting in the morning.

Nate had vowed to stay in the valley as long as it took to bring the panther to bay. The discovery of the dead warrior had fueled his resolve. But was he being realistic? How long would it take to hunt Satan down? Another day? Two? A week? A month? He'd seen how easily the cat could elude him. Unless the animal walked right up to him and begged to be shot or he was extraordinarily lucky, he might end up wasting a lot of time and energy and have nothing to show for it.

Nate knew that Shakespeare didn't agree with his plan and was only staying because of their deep friendship. Such devotion was rare, which made him appreciate McNair's feelings all the more and caused him to question whether he had the right to endanger his friend's life to satisfy his personal sense of justice.

What to do? Nate asked himself. He mounted and headed down the mountain, casting frequent glances at the cliffs in the vain hope of spying Satan.

The glow of a beckoning fire served as a beacon and brought Nate right to the camp as twilight blanketed the countryside in a gray mantle. Shakespeare was whittling and looked up but made no comment. Wearily, Nate stripped off his saddle and took a seat.

"I don't need to ask how it went."

"Give me another day," Nate said.

"That's all? I thought we were sticking until we have the painter's pelt."

"I wanted to, but I had a chance to do some thinking today. And it wouldn't be fair to you."

"There you go again."

"What?"

"Using that favorite word of yours." Shakespeare stroked his keen knife into the piece of broken tree limb he held, carving off a chip. "Don't worry about what's fair for me. If you want to kill this cat, we kill it. Simple as that." He stared at the younger trapper. "This above all, to thine own self be true. And it must follow, as the night the day, thou canst not then be false to any man."

"It's hard, sometimes, being true to our convictions," Nate commented.

"Health to you, valiant sir."

"Why do you say that?"

"Mine honor keeps the weather of my fate. Life every man holds dear, but the dear man holds honor far more precious-dear than life."

"Are you saying that about me or about yourself?" Nate asked.

McNair chuckled and quoted more of the Bard of Avon. "Here's Agamemnon, an honest fellow enough and one that loves quails, but he has not so much brain as ear wax."

To divert his friend from the subject at hand, Nate nodded at the limb being whittled. "What is that you're making? It looks to me like a stake of some kind?"

"I rest my case," Shakespeare said softly. Then, in a normal tone, he answered, "Very perceptive, Horatio. It's a stake of the only kind." Shifting, he revealed a pile of five additional stakes lying behind him.

"What are they for?"

"Your feline friend," Shakespeare said. "I've lived in these mountains a long time, so long I know them as well as city folks in the States know their puny back yards. I know all the animals that live in these mountains, including painters. So I wasn't too surprised when you showed up empty-handed." He resumed shaping the stake. "Grizzlies have reputations for being the fiercest beasts in the Rockies, and wolverines are known for their cunning and savagery, but in this old coon's humble opinion neither can hold a candle to a riled panther."

"How will a bunch of stakes help us kill Satan?"

"Think, son," Shakespeare said. "You're tired, that's plain to see, but use that noodle of yours." He hefted the stake he was working on. "Once, years ago, a glutton snuck into a Flathead village and made off with a little baby. The father decided he was going to kill that wolverine come Hell or high water. He tried everything. Tracking, hunting from horseback, setting out bait and hiding nearby, but none of his ideas worked. One day he dug himself a pit, lined the bottom with a lot of stakes, and covered the pit with thin branches, grass, and leaves. He made the covering strong enough to hold the weight of a fawn he killed, which he gutted and laid out as pretty as you please for the wolverine to find. Then he went on back to his lodge."

"Did the glutton fall for it?"

Shakespeare laughed. "I'll never poke fun at your wit again." He nodded. "Yep. The very next day he went back and found that wolverine turned into the hairiest pincushion you ever did see."

"So you're fixing to do the same with Satan?"

"I have to do something useful," Shakespeare said.

"While you're off gallivanting around tomorrow, I'll begin on the pit. If you haven't rubbed Satan out in a day or two, maybe we should try the Flathead's way."

"I'm game," Nate said.

McNair chortled merrily. "Twice in one minute. You're on a roll, Nathaniel. You truly are."

Smiling, Nate idly gazed into the fire at the blazing wood, and suddenly vivid, painful memories of another time and another place blanked everything else from his mind.

The shed smelled of dank earth and freshly chopped wood. Propped in one corner was a large axe. To one side, piled chest high, was the wood the family used in their fireplace.

Nate stood facing the rear wall, leaning forward with his arms bracing his weight. He heard his father moving behind him and tensed for the first blow.

"I warned you, didn't I? I told you that you're never too old for me to give you a licking?"

"Yes."

"Yes, what?"

"Yes, sir."

"The next time I tell you to do something, maybe you'll see fit to do it. I won't tolerate being disobeyed, not by you or any of your brothers."

"The doves wasn't hurting anyone, Father. I saw no reason to kill them."

"I explained all that to you when you first objected," the elder King said with exaggerated patience. "Those doves were sitting in that tree every morning and evening, getting their droppings all over the flower bed. Disgusting birds! We shooed them off time and again but they kept coming back. All you had to do was hide around the corner with that bow Zeke gave you and put an arrow into one or both of them. Was that too much to ask?"

"I won't kill an innocent dove, not for you, not for anyone."

"Do you know what this reminds me of? That time two years ago when you gave me so much trouble over killing a few filthy mice and some pesky cats. Do you remember?"

"I've never forgotten it."

"Then I'd think you should have learned an important lesson. Sherman took care of those cats for me, just like he took care of the doves when you wouldn't. What good did being so stubborn get you? The doves still died."

"I'll only kill when *I* think it's right, Father. And I don't care whether it's a mouse or a bird or a deer."

"Where did I go wrong with you?"

Nate made no reply. There were swishing sounds to his rear as his father swung the strap to warm up.

"I regret having to discipline you, son. I truly do. But you leave me no other choice."

Still Nate did not answer.

"I will not abide being treated with disrespect," his father snapped. "Respect is the most important part of any relationship."

"I thought it was love," Nate finally spoke.

The next moment the strap bit into him. He arched his back and ground his teeth together, refusing to give his father the satisfaction of seeing him cry. Not this time! Not ever again! Wincing with each blow, he mentally counted them off: "One, two, three, four, five, six, seven. . . ."

And on and on it went.

Chapter Twelve

In the rosy blush of blazing dawn the sheer cliffs changed from their typical dull brown hue to a bright flesh-colored tint, seeming to come alive, to glisten with vitality.

Nate King sat astride the black stallion, his gaze roving over the high ramparts as he diligently sought a clue to Satan's whereabouts. The panther had not shown itself during the night, much to his disappointment. He'd stayed up late just in case the cat did, and now he felt the lingering effects of having gone without a decent night's sleep.

Stifling a yawn, Nate rode eastward. Yesterday he had checked the west end of the cliffs; today he would scout in the opposite direction. A piece of jerky served as breakfast. He had been in too much of a hurry to partake of the fine flapjacks Shakespeare had been preparing when he left.

Nate regretted being so impetuous. His stomach growled without letup and he craved a hot cup of coffee. Well, he reflected, what's done was done and he might as well buckle down to the matter at hand.

An animal appeared high above, then another, and another, all moving with fearless precision along the cliff face, bounding from outcropping to ledge to shelf. At times they were balanced on knobs of rock no bigger than a man's fist. Yet they were as sure-footed in their element as a mule would be on terra firma.

"Bighorns," Nate said to himself. One day soon he was going to honor a promise and take his son Zach bighorn hunting. The elusive creatures were prized for their taste, which most mountain men compared favorably to that of mutton. Many claimed bighorn meat was tastier and juicier. A few trappers made it a point early each spring, when the bighorns inhabited lower elevations because of deep snow on the crags, to bring one of the animals down and hold a grand feast. Nate had been to one of the raucous affairs, and it was there he'd first savored a bighorn steak. He couldn't wait to enjoy another.

But today the presence of the bighorns above was bothersome since it meant Satan wasn't in the area. Nate trotted on along the base of the cliffs, alternating his attention between the heights and the ground.

Midmorning found Nate at a place where a dozen or so boulders had fallen from on high. He ground-hitched the stallion, carried his parfleche to a rock slab on which he took a seat, and pulled the last piece of pemmican out. A few more hours and he would have traveled the entire length of the cliffs. If he didn't spot Satan by then, he was inclined to call off the search and give McNair's pit a try. It couldn't hurt.

Nate chewed and thought and didn't realize several minutes had gone by until the strident screech of a bird of prey drew his interest to a bald eagle soaring on the uplifting air currents. He watched the eagle sail in a small circle, then swoop at the crest. Again and again it did the same thing.

Intrigued, Nate hopped off the slab and stepped backward until he had a clear view of the top. The eagle would dive at the rim, flap its wings a few times, then swerve aside, regain altitude, and repeat the behavior. Either it was trying to snare a small animal, or it was trying to drive something off. But what could be up that high, Nate mused, other than a bighorn or a marmot?

Inspiration jarred Nate to his core. Wheeling, he sprinted to the stallion and mounted. A hard ride brought him to where the cliffs came to an end. Swinging around the rock wall, he saw a gradual slope leading up toward the summit.

The eagle was gone but Nate wasn't taking anything for granted. He grasped the Hawken in his left hand, the stock supported by his thigh. As usual the ground was too packed to bear prints although he did come on a smudged print that resembled a cat's.

It was well past noon when Nate found large black and white feathers scattered over a small area near the rim. Close by was a short tree in which the second eagle had probably been perched when set upon. A trail of feathers led upward.

Nate cocked the rifle and warily advanced. So far as he knew, panthers rarely attacked eagles. The bald variety, and the golden kind too, was formidable when provoked. Satan had to be very hungry to risk having his eyes gouged out.

The feathers were spaced at irregular intervals. Presently they led Nate to what appeared to be a wide cleft. Sliding off the stallion, he squatted near the edge and peered downward. The ghastly sight below made him recoil in astonishment.

At one time the ground had cracked and split wide, forming a thirty foot trough extending northward from the cliff rim. Littering the bottom of this trough were jumbled bones piled three feet high. Buffalo bones, deer bones, bighorn bones, they were all there. So were those of marmots, badgers, ferrets, beavers, raccoons, opossums, and assorted smaller animals. In the midst of the tangled mass lay the skull of a small horse.

Nate blinked, then leaned over the edge. He had never seen so many skeletons collected in one spot. They were a morbid record of Satan's kills over the past decade, or longer. Easing onto the grade below, he stepped carefully to the pile and picked up the leg bone of a buffalo calf. As he did, he noticed a human skull among the assortment.

Quickly Nate pried the skull loose to study it. The victim had been a child, judging by the size, most likely a boy. It was very old, proving Satan had been a confirmed man-killer years ago.

A sudden scratching, as of claws on rock, reminded Nate of the peril in which he had put himself. He quietly set the boy's skull down and turned toward the mouth of the trough. Was it his imagination or did a shadow flit across the opening?

Hawken leveled, Nate crept to the crest of the cliff. Here the trough angled lower into a funnel shaped hole in the stone surface large enough to permit a steam engine to pass through. From lower down on the mountain the opening would have been impossible to spot.

Sliding on his backside, Nate worked his way toward the hole. He felt confident, alert. His left foot hurt just a bit and his rib ached dully, otherwise he felt fine. Near the hole the rock surface flattened, enabling him to squat and peek into a dimly lit cave.

He'd done it! Nate had found Satan's den! Now that he had, there was the question of how to flush Satan out so he could end the monster's vicious reign of terror. An eight or nine foot drop would take him to the dusty floor, which wasn't much of a drop at all, but landing would aggravate his left leg and might throw him off balance, giving the panther the opening it needed to pounce on him before he could snap off a shot.

Then, too, there was no way back out that Nate could see. Once down there, he'd starve to death if Satan didn't get him first, and he didn't care to end his days on such an ignoble note after having gone to so much trouble. Unfortunately, he hadn't thought to bring a rope along. Nate straightened, hefted the Hawken, and debated whether to tell Shakespeare of his discovery so they could work out a plan together.

A bloodcurdling snarl erupted directly above. Spinning, Nate glanced up and beheld his worst nightmare come true.

Satan was poised on the rim of the trough, the dead eagle hanging limply from his mighty jaws, dry blood plastering his chin. The panther's eyes were alight with primal fury. His sanctuary had been violated by the frail creature he had tried to kill several times without success, and the entrance to his haven was blocked. His inherent bloodlust swelled, dominating his being, and he took a stride nearer.

Nate was in dire straits. He couldn't retreat very far with the cliff rim at his back. Nor could he go more than a few feet to the right or the left. His sole avenue of escape was up the funnel to the trough, and Satan had him cut off. He fingered the hammer of his rifle, hesitant to shoot for fear of provoking the panther into charging since even if he killed it, the beast's momentum might knock him back over the edge or into the hole.

What else could he do, though? Nate realized, and jammed the stock to his shoulder. As he did, Satan dropped the eagle, snarled, and sprang. Then everything happened so fast, Nate had no time to react. The Hawken boomed, a cloud of gunsmoke bloomed, preventing Nate from seeing the onrushing cat, and the next heartbeat he was sent flying by a heavy impact on his shoulder. Frantically he flailed his arms, seeking a purchase, but there was none.

The shock of smashing down on his back whooshed the air from Nate's lungs. Above him he saw the cave opening, saw Satan's head appear and heard the mountain lion vent its rage with a rumbling growl.

Nate scrambled to his feet and backed away. Somehow he had kept his hold on the rifle. Holding it in his left hand, he drew a pistol, aimed it at the feline's feral visage, and cocked the piece. Satan promptly vanished.

Halting, Nate wedged the flintlock under his belt again and hurriedly commenced reloading the Hawken. He glanced at his surroundings and learned the cave was much bigger than he had thought, so big, in fact, it qualified as a cavern.

From outside came more growling. Nate's fingers flew. When the rifle was ready, he slid the ramrod into its housing and leaned against the rock wall to catch his breath.

The temporary respite gave Nate the opportunity to study the cavern closely. Enough sunshine poured through the gaping entrance to bathe the interior in light for a score of yards in all directions. Beyond the radius of the sunlight, to the east, reared bulky shadows, boulders, Nate guessed.

The floor was level where Nate stood and in the middle, where he had fallen, but on the east side it seemed to angle downward. The walls were smooth, as was the ceiling. There were no stalagmites or stalactites.

Nate focused on the opening. Sooner or later Satan would see fit to jump down after him. His wisest recourse, then, was to wait there and put a ball in the panther's brain when it did. Accordingly, he inched nearer to the center of the chamber.

The growling above had ceased.

Butterflies fluttered in Nate's stomach and he tried to calm his nerves by sheer force of will. He licked his dry lips, then stared at the east end of the cavern. Those bulky shapes were clearer now, and he saw that they were broken chunks of rock of varying sizes, some taller than he was, evidently all that was left of a toppled wall.

Where was Satan? Nate wondered. Why wasn't the panther coming in to get him? He walked directly under the rim and craned his neck for a glimpse of the lion or its shadow but saw neither.

After five minutes elapsed and there was no activity above, Nate moved to the other side of the hole, cautiously keeping out of sight. The new angle proved no better. Puzzled, he cast about on the floor and found a suitable rock which he then threw upward. It clattered noisily but failed to spark a response.

Nate didn't know what to make of this development. He didn't believe Satan would simply wander off, not when he occupied the panther's lair. Was it biding its time, waiting up there for him? Or—and here a new idea hit him—was there another way into the cavern, a way only Satan knew?

Venturing into the murky realm fringing the entrance, where the floor angled gradually downward, Nate came on piles of earth and heaps of stones, additional residue from the crumbled wall. There were more huge boulders than he had imagined, and he threaded his way among them with supreme care.

The cavern turned out to be enormous. Beyond the boulders the floor became level again. No sunlight filtered through, but Nate's eyes had adjusted sufficiently to the dark to enable him to distinguish inky outlines. He walked forward taking small steps, testing his footing before applying his whole weight. Caves often contained nasty surprises such as crevices and pits, and he didn't want to blunder into one.

Nate had gone over fifty feet by his reckoning when a soft puff of air struck his cheek. He halted, elated. A breeze meant there was another opening somewhere near, perhaps a means of reaching the outer world. Turning this way and that he tried to pinpoint which direction the breeze came from.

Satisfied the answer was off to the right, Nate worked toward a wall. It appeared solid enough, and there were no telltale points of light. Had he erred? No, because another whisper of air caressed his face, a little stronger this time.

Stopping, Nate ran his hand over the rough surface, feeling for a crack or a concealed passage. He moved to the left and squatted to check lower down. Immediately a blast of wind hit him head-on.

What was this? Nate asked himself excitedly. Groping over a wide area, he discovered a ragged hole the size of a melon. Through this the breeze wafted.

Nate kept searching in the hope there was another opening, one big enough for him to crawl through. But there wasn't, and in his frustration he clenched his fist and swore under his breath.

Hugging the wall, Nate sought another way out. He refused to give up, refused to give Satan the satisfaction of prevailing. A troubling thought occurred to him a few yards farther on: What if Satan was smart enough to know that he would eventually succumb to hunger and thirst? What if the panther had no intention of coming in after him until assured he was good and dead?

That couldn't be the case, Nate reflected. There wasn't a mountain lion alive that smart, that clever. He kept looking, searching every nook and cranny, making a complete circuit without finding the yearned after escape route.

Suppressing an impulse to panic, Nate returned to the entrance. The sunshine sparkled as it fell through the hole, lending the setting an enchanted aspect like in a child's fairy tale. But there was nothing enchanting about the certain fate awaiting Nate unless he found a way out of the trap in which he had unwittingly put himself.

A turtle-shaped boulder offered a tempting seat. Nate loosened the pistols for instant use and studied the rim nine feet up. How the dickens was he going to reach that high to pull himself out? He couldn't very well sprout wings or build a ladder. And he couldn't jump with his leg in the shape it was in.

The turtle-shaped boulder gave Nate a brainstorm when he slapped it in annoyance, stinging his palm. He looked down at it, frowned, then drew back as if it had slapped him in the face in return. Of course! he mused. Why hadn't he thought of it sooner?

Hurriedly Nate moved about, seeking boulders light enough to lift and flat enough to be stacked one on top of the other. Right away he located two and lugged them under the rim, wincing as his hurt rib protested the exertion. One more brought the height to just over two feet.

Nate gauged the distance to the edge of the entrance and nodded. Climbing onto the top boulder, he perched like a hawk about to take flight. The top of the hole was less than a foot above his head. All he had to do was jump and seize hold. Only one thing stopped him, uncertainty over Satan's whereabouts. Nate would be totally helpless for the few seconds he hung there before climbing up, and in that span Satan could take his head off with a single swipe.

Nate jumped down and went in search of another flat boulder. He had to look longer this time, but he found one and added it to his stack. Now when he stood on the top he could straighten high enough to see over the lip. Still, he paused, straining his ears to catch any sounds. A growl, heavy breathing, the pad of paws, anything.

The deep silence was unnerving. Nate slowly rose on his toes and risked peeking out. To his amazement, Satan was nowhere to be seen, not in the area of the funnel nor in the part of the trough visible from the entrance. Inexplicably, the panther had gone away.

Nate didn't waste another moment. Resting the Hawken on the lip in front of him, he placed both palms flat, coiled his shoulders, and shoved upward. Once on firm footing, he grabbed the rifle and dashed up the incline into the trough and from there out onto open ground. Still, Satan didn't show.

To say Nate was happy was the understatement of the century. He had stared death in the face, as it were, yet again, and lived to tell the tale. Maybe Shakespeare was right. Maybe he did have more luck than most two men combined.

Grinning at his deliverance, Nate turned to mount the black stallion and did a double take on finding the horse gone. A few partial prints told the story. Satan had tried to bring the stallion down, but the powerful black had fought back and fled with the mountain lion in earnest pursuit.

So now Nate knew why Satan hadn't been waiting outside the cavern. He began running, pacing himself so he wouldn't become fatigued too quickly, anxiously seeking sign of his horse and the cat. Thankfully he was going downhill.

Nate covered hundreds of yards before a sharp pang in his side compelled him to rest briefly. Striding to the crown of the cliff, he gazed in reverent awe out over the magnificent expanse of verdant countryside unfurled below the heights. On his way up he had been so intent on spotting tracks, he hadn't paid all that much attention to the tremendous view.

Nate swore he could see almost to the broad Mississippi. Majestic mountains mingled with rolling emerald hills to the north and the south, forming undulating waves that grew smaller with distance. A sea of verdant forest covered most of the landscape, except for brown breakers where stark peaks and cliffs such as the one he was on reared skyward. Far, far to the east, at the very horizon, lay a stretch of grassy flatland like a green shoreline, perhaps the prairie itself.

Movement below shattered Nate's contemplation of Nature's awesome grandeur. He spied the black stallion making for woods flanking the heights. Satan still gave chase but was hopelessly outdistanced.

Nate continued jogging. His foot began aching terribly, and not to be outdone, his rib did the same. Regardless, he forged on, oblivious to everything except the need to save the stallion. Often he had to slow to allow his foot and chest to stop throbbing.

The afternoon waxed, waned.

On the brink of exhaustion, Nate halted close to the bottom of the cliffs, within an eighth of a mile of the forest into which the stallion had gone. Dripping with sweat, he sat on a rock and collected his strength for the next spurt. He looked up, saw the long shadow of an isolated tree spearing at him, and realized how very late it had become. Shifting, he was troubled to note the sun had partially dipped from sight. Twilight was minutes off.

From the frying pan into the fire, as the old saying went. Nate rose and hastened toward the trees. At least there he could find shelter, find a spot to hide until daylight, hopefully somewhere that offered some protection from the panther.

Nate knew that Satan would be on his heels eventually. Once the mountain lion gave up its pursuit of the stallion, it would venture back and pick up his scent. He had to be in a defensible position before it caught up.

The shadows of the foremost phalanx of pines formed a dark band on the paler grass. They blanketed Nate as he came to the forest and entered their gloomy dominion. An eerie quiet gripped the woods, a bad omen.

Nate found the stallion's tracks readily enough and trailed them. It was doubtful he could overtake the horse before nightfall closed in, but he would try. He didn't care to spend the night in the woods if he could help it.

To the west the sun sank steadily, painting the sky brilliant streaks of red, orange, and pink. The northwesterly wind increased, as always. To the south an elk trumpeted, a rare sound at that time of year.

Nate crept anxiously along, his grip on the Hawken

as steely as the gleam in his eyes. More than ever he burned with a desire to put an end to Satan, to give the panther a small measure of its due for those who had fallen prey to its insatiable butchery. Satan was a deviate specimen, a freak of Nature, a lion that lived for the pure joy of slaughter rather than to merely fill its belly when hungry.

Suddenly Nate stopped, his eyes widening.

Coming toward him was the feline terror.

Chapter Thirteen

Nate King was filled with fleeting shock on seeing the scourge of the Rockies not fifty feet off. Satan had spied him the same moment he had spied the panther and, voicing a guttural snarl, the mountain lion bore down on him at incredible speed. Nate cocked the rifle and snapped off a shot, in his haste neglecting to aim properly. At the blast Satan swerved into the undergrowth and was swallowed by the gloom.

Whirling, Nate ran, fleeing in uncontrolled fear. He went only a few yards when shame brought him up short. Turning, he whipped out a pistol, then stepped to the side to a fir tree. Low branches provided firm purchase, and in seconds he had climbed twenty feet and was squatting in the fork of a pair of thick limbs.

Nate glimpsed a tawny coat to the east and took precise aim, but Satan wasn't staying in one place. The panther blended into a thicket. Although Nate scoured the vegetation intently, he saw no trace of the big cat.

Now what should he do? Nate quizzed himself. The lion had him treed, effectively trapped again, just like in the cavern. Only this time his stallion wasn't close at hand to lure the panther elsewhere. And this time Satan could spring at him from any direction, at any time. His being in the tree made little difference to a predator capable of scaling the vertical trunk and reaching him in two swift leaps.

Nate set the flintlock at his feet and rapidly reloaded the rifle, stopping only once when a twig cracked behind him. He spun to see if Satan was sneaking up on him. Breath bated, he scanned the plant growth, saw a chipmunk scampering from cover to cover. Thus reassured, he finished ramming the ball and patch into the barrel.

All that remained of the setting sun was a crimson crown. A spreading pall of darkness obscured the landscape, and the shadows were now themselves in deeper shadow. Soon the moon would rise.

Replacing the pistol under his belt, Nate sat, his legs curled under him. If he was Satan, he'd wait until night had the forest firmly in its inky grip before attacking, but panthers were known for being unpredictable. Satan might not want to wait that long.

Nate peered upward, marking the positions of limbs. With a bit of luck he'd be able to climb another twenty feet. After that the branches were spaced too far apart.

The only problem with going higher was that the limbs higher up were thinner, less able to bear Nate's weight. And nowhere was there as wide a fork as the one supporting him. Better, he reasoned, to stay right where he was and bide his time until the panther made a move.

Nate rubbed his eyes and fought a yawn. He'd been up since well before dawn and had not partaken of food or water since the night before. Since his parfleche was on the stallion, he'd have to do without a while longer.

The heavens dimmed to black; the canopy of blue gave way to an indigo canopy sprinkled with sparkling pinpoints. In the east blossomed the gleaming moon, bathing the Rockies in its iridescent light. A coyote greeted its advent with a wavering howl and was answered by another elsewhere.

Holding the Hawken on his knees, Nate leaned forward, bending low over one of the branches in order to make it harder for the panther to distinguish him from the tree. A flutter of wings to the west heralded the flight of a large owl, and Nate watched as the aerial artist looped upward and was silhouetted against the radiant lunar surface.

Typical night sounds reached Nate's ears: the lonesome wails of wolves, the snort of a black-tailed buck as it fled on smelling Satan's scent, the grunt of a roving grizzly to the southwest. Noticeably lacking was any sound made by Satan, which did not bode well for Nate. His skin pricked as if from a rash, and he had the sensation of being spied on by unseen eyes. But try as he might, he couldn't locate the panther.

Nate had to change position after an hour due to a cramp in his left leg. He tried to do so noiselessly but his left legging scraped the branch loud enough to be heard yards away.

There was plenty of time for Nate to think, about Shakespeare, about Winona, about Zach, and his daughter, Evelyn, and how each time he braved the wilderness he gambled his life that he would ever see them again. The wilderness was a harsh taskmaster. Those who survived the lessons it taught were those who never let their guard down for a moment.

Mountain Cat

Was it worth it? Nate speculated. Was it worth being a free trapper when he stood to lose everyone and everything he truly loved every time he went up against a bestial nightmare like Satan or tangled with a war party of hostile Indians? Was the pure, precious freedom he enjoyed living in the wilderness worth the price he might have to pay for it?

There could only be one answer: Yes! A million times, yes! Freedom was worth any price. Not the watered-down kind of freedom found back in the States where politicians conspired to dictate how people should live, but true freedom, that personal state where men and women could live as they damn well pleased without being accountable to anyone other than their Maker.

Such thoughts, and many others, occupied Nate for some time. Two more hours went by, then a third. The moon climbed steadily. Nate yawned frequently and fought off an urge to sleep.

About midnight Nate found himself dozing fitfully off and on. His leaden eyes would close, his chin would sag, then he would realize what he was doing, jerk his head up, and try to stay awake until the next time.

Nate probed the nearby vegetation over and over but did not see the panther. By about three in the morning he began to suspect that Satan had left and there was no need for him to remain vigilant. Fatigue eclipsed his caution, and despite his intentions, he slipped into a deep slumber.

Nate would never know what awakened him. One moment he was asleep, the next his eyes were open and it was much lighter than he remembered it being and he was staring at one of the limbs forming the fork in which he sat and there on the limb, crouched low, ears drawn back, was Satan. .

The instant Nate saw the panther, Satan sprang. Nate clutched the Hawken and tried to bring it to bear but his sleep-dulled reflexes were much too sluggish. Satan slammed into the rifle, batting it loose with a single sweep of an iron paw, and landed on the limb inches from the fork, close enough to disembowel Nate with the next stroke.

Only Nate wasn't there any longer. He threw himself backward and deliberately let himself fall, taking the chance he wouldn't break his neck hitting a branch on the way down. A jolting impact lanced his hip with agony, then he was falling again. He hit the ground hard, rolled, and rose to one knee.

Satan was already in midair, snarling fiercely, claws extended.

Nate took a hasty bead. His finger was constricting on the trigger when the mountain lion plowed into him with the force of a battering ram, sending him tumbling. He felt his shirt rip, felt blood drawn. But the new wound was far from fatal, and when Nate stopped tumbling he pushed to his feet and grabbed at his pistols. His arms twin blurs, he drew and aimed and cocked and fired, just as Satan reached him. The twin balls bowled the cat rearward but it was up in a flash and pressing its attack.

A paw nearly took Nate's leg off at the knee. He retreated, throwing the pistols at Satan's head, making the panther duck and giving him the opportunity to grasp both his butcher knife and his tomahawk. Then Satan closed in.

Now the fight was joined in earnest. There was no time for Nate to think, no time for him to plot a means of beating the monster, no time for anything other than simply staying alive, for preserving his life as best he was able.

Satan came in low, trying to bring Nate down by tearing into his legs. Nate countered with a wicked slash of the tomahawk that drove Satan to one side. The panther spun, angled in again, and was again driven back by a flick of the butcher knife. Baffled, the lion stood still a few moments, growling and hissing.

Nate lunged, aiming a tomahawk blow at the panther's skull. In doing so he noticed a recent gash where he had struck the cat by the stream days ago. Evidently Satan remembered too, because the mountain lion wanted no part of the tomahawk. Whenever Nate swung it, the panther darted aside, giving the weapon a wide berth.

Satan started circling, walking swiftly, steely body hugging the ground, tail snaking back and forth. Every so often Satan would swipe a paw as if probing for weakness. Nate had to keep turning in order to keep facing the feline fury. When the panther swung, so did he, holding Satan at bay.

The stalemate lasted minutes. Nate's blood raced, his temples pounded. He didn't need to be told what would happen if he made a single small mistake. Satan would be on him before he could blink, tearing his flesh from his body. No matter what, he must not blunder!

But he did.

It happened in this fashion: Nate was turning, always turning, inadvertently bearing to the left as he did, his gaze locked on the panther to the exclusion of everything else, and so it was that he failed to see a short sapling growing right under his nose until, as he pivoted yet one more time on his heel, his foot bumped into the obstacle and he tripped, tripped *forward*, toward the panther.

Satan recoiled, but not quite quickly enough to evade Nate's knife which by sheer chance speared into Satan's left eye. Nate came down on all fours, saw Satan tense, and barely got the tomahawk up before the mountain lion leaped. The edge of the tomahawk bit into Satan's face but hardly slowed the enraged beast. Nate was bowled over, the cat on top, his tomahawk arm under the panther's chin as he desperately tried to stop Satan's razor teeth from finding his throat. Claws tore his shirt, his leggings. In desperation Nate plunged his long knife into Satan's side, over and over and over.

Without warning Satan jumped off, whirled, and came at Nate again. Nate attempted to rise, to meet the rush standing, but his speed compared to that of the savage feline was as that of a tortoise to a hare. He thrust the knife, burying the blade to the hilt, as the panther bowled him over. By a quirk of fate he wound up flush against Satan's side so he looped an arm around the lion's thick neck and held tight while simultaneously stabbing again and again and again.

Satan became a whirlwind, spinning and flipping and clawing in a frenzied bid to shake the tormentor off. Nate clung on for dear life, stabbing, stabbing, always stabbing. He nearly lost his grip when they rolled into a tree or a boulder. Fangs sank into his shoulder, causing him to cry out. The next moment, there in front of him, was Satan's other eye, and as the lion drew back, he rammed the blade into it.

No one could have held onto the panther after that. Satan erupted into a berserk rage, twisting and jumping and rolling as if demented. Nate lost his grip on both the knife and the lion and flew through the air, smacking against a pine. Sitting up, he was startled to discover he had lost the tomahawk. He pushed upright, empty-handed, defenseless, and backed against the tree, prepared to sell his life dearly even though he was feeling weak and faint.

Abruptly, Satan emitted a high-pitched shriek and vaulted straight up into the air, clawing at the emptiness in a last act of ferocious defiance. Then Satan crashed down, convulsed, and was still.

Nate gaped at his bestial foe, unable to believe his own eyes. He took a halting step, searching for the Hawken and the pistols, when suddenly a wave of vertigo brought him low, buckling his legs and pitching him onto his face. The last sight he saw was a patch of grass sweeping toward him.

The pungent scent of wood smoke brought Nate around. He sniffed, opened his eyes, and went to sit up, stopping when he found a blanket covered him to his chin and realized he was propped on a saddle. His own saddle.

"Glad you could join the world of the living."

Nate stared across the fire at his mentor. "You?" he croaked. "How?"

"How else? I was a mite worried when you didn't show for supper so I came looking for you. Had to track by torchlight, which is as hard as the dickens to do unless you know what you're doing. I was up on the cliffs when I heard shots." Shakespeare poured coffee into a tin cup and brought it over. "I found you this morning about dawn."

The afternoon sun told Nate how long he had been unconscious. "Thanks for coming after me."

I'm just glad I found you when I did. You lost a lot of blood, son. You're damned lucky to be alive."

"Where did you find the stallion?"

"I didn't. It came wandering into camp about the middle of the morning." Shakespeare handed over the cup. "Careful. That's hot."

Nodding absently, Nate took a slow sip. "It's over," he said softly.

"Sure is. I skinned the painter for you." Shakespeare grinned. "'Course, the pelt won't amount to much with all the holes you put in it." He gently touched Nate's brow. "There's no fever. Do you feel all right?"

Nate King felt the warmth in his belly from the delicious coffee, felt the wind in his hair and the pleasant sunshine on his face, and he smiled in heartfelt contentment. "Never better, my friend. Never better."